KINGS ROW

Winner of the Blue Mountain Novel Award

Hidden River Arts offers the **Blue Mountain Novel Award** for an original, unpublished novel of any length. The award provides $1,000 and publication by Hidden River Publishing on its Hidden River Press imprint.

Hidden River Arts is an interdisciplinary arts organization dedicated to supporting and celebrating the unserved artists among us, particularly those outside the artistic and academic mainstream.

PRAISE FOR

KINGS ROW

"In the utterly absorbing *Kings Row*, Jeffrey Voccola shows himself to be a master of the faultlines of class and of all the ways, large and small, in which people hurt each other. I couldn't stop turning the pages of this suspenseful novel. *Kings Row* is a stellar debut."

> —MARGOT LIVESEY, author of *Mercury* and *The House on Fortune Street*

"This beautifully-paced, eloquent and suspenseful novel is full of persuasive, sharply observed psychology, sociology, and topology, and an honest voicing of working class people, male and female. Set in an upstate Pennsylvania university town, as distinct from nearby farm and rust belt towns and from the middle- and upper-class worlds of Philadelphia's suburbs, the primary characters are young adults at the breaking point of their lives and destinies. Given a shocking murder—"things like this didn't happen. Not in Waylan. Not here"—there are no villains. There is both humanity and pathos throughout, and sympathy with conflicting perspectives. Voccola writes with dead-pan lyricism, an attentive ear, and generous heart."

> —DEWITT HENRY, author of *Sweet Marjoram* and co-founder of *Ploughshares*

"From its masterful opening chapter on, *Kings Row* captures the divides and resentments that have brought us to this moment in America. This novel is a deep study of people unsure of their positions in their personal lives and in the larger sphere of change. Voccola writes beautifully and compassionately, even about tragedy. His eye for the details and psyches of working-class people, and for all people beset by alienation and uncertainty, is as good as any writer's I know. The sense of place is undeniably specific, yet also universal. *Kings Row* is a novel of incisive observation and profound understanding from a writer who immerses us in his moving, fictional world with every word."

—TIM PARRISH, author of *Fear and What Follows:
The Violent Education of a Christian Racist, A Memoir*

"*Kings Row* masterfully deconstructs a killing deeply emblematic of the class and race issues that plague our time. With lyrical, heart-piercing realism, Jeffrey Voccola evokes our deepest compassion for these ill-fated characters, showing us ourselves reflected in college students struggling to belong, in displaced working class communities. Provocative and suspenseful, *Kings Row* introduces an exciting new writer to watch."

—WAYNE HARRISON, author of *The Spark and the Drive*
and *Wrench and Other Stories*

KINGS ROW

JEFFREY VOCCOLA

HIDDEN RIVER PRESS
Philadelphia   2020

The chapter "Returns" was originally published in *The Woven Tale Press*,
Vol. VII, No. 6 (2019), 86.

Cover design by Lesley MacLean
Interior design and typography by P. M. Gordon Associates

Library of Congress Control Number: 2020930452
ISBN 978-0-9994915-4-6

HIDDEN RIVER PRESS
An imprint of Hidden River Publishing
Philadelphia, Pennsylvania

CONTENTS

KINGS ROW

WAYLAN

H E WAS FOUND on the sidewalk outside Jon Bishop's hardware store, curled on his side as if he were sleeping. One of his sneakers had come off and a girl was kneeling beside him trying to put it back on his foot. Other students stood in the road, holding their foreheads as they spoke into cell phones.

This was how it was described to Doris Weidner, who owned Petal Pushers two buildings down. She got the call early the following morning, only a few hours after it'd happened. Doris liked to be in the shop by five-thirty so she could put out fresh displays in time for the morning traffic, and when the phone rang she hesitated. Calls at that hour always startled her; only the weight of bad news could move a person to interrupt the calm of early morning. She held her hand over the phone, flexed the stiffness from her fingers before finally lifting the receiver.

On the line was her son Ronald, a patrol officer with the Willowbrook County Police Department almost fifteen years now.

"It was right outside your place," he said. His voice fluttered with excitement, as if this made Waylan important. "The first murder Waylan has seen in almost a century. Can you believe that?"

The news sent tremors through Doris's body. These students. She complained about them sometimes. They came to Waylan each year in a gridlocked parade of minivans and U-haul trucks: girls tanned and slender, boys with wide bands of perspiration down their backs. During the day they hung out at the coffee shop and on their front stoops, and when the bars let out on Thursday nights you could hear them grab-assing their way back to the dorms.

There was a time when the university wasn't a problem, but these kids came from all over now, from outside Pennsylvania, from cities. There were Blacks and Hispanics in town, kids with hairstyles and a swagger too urban for a community this small, getting sideways looks from the old Dutchies. It seemed like the university extended its reach a little farther into town each year. Many of the farms had been bought and developed; dormitories were popping up everywhere. There was even talk of taking the fairgrounds, which has been here over a hundred years.

Doris still had great love for her hometown, the narrow streets and pretty front lawns, the three-story homes with original pine floors and rotary light switches. There were antique stores and secondhand shops on Main Street and an ice cream parlor that looked straight out of the 1950s. And there were the Amish, who drove horse-drawn carriages along the main drag. They lived on a six-hundred acre swath of land less than five miles from Waylan, right off of Route 25. Sometimes the Amish girls rode their bikes through town, pedaling straight-backed as the hem of their dresses fluttered in the wind.

Doris paced around the shop listening to the floorboards pop and creak beneath her feet. She felt a draft that made her cinch the belt of her sweater a little tighter. Through the front window she could see the traffic starting to pick up, the sway of tree limbs. Stretched across the lamp posts was a banner for the new Owen Turner exhibit at the university. Owen had grown up in Waylan. Doris remembered him as a boy, small and timid, odd, and she still felt a knot of pride in her throat whenever she heard his name mentioned on television. He left Waylan in the 1980s and it was said he lived on the New York City streets for a while, but it wasn't long before his artwork meant something to people. When she first heard he had become famous Doris prayed for him, that he wouldn't fall to sin. She knew about temptation and Owen didn't seem like the sort who could fend it off.

There is a sculpture of Owen's in the park, a tall, faceless abstract of a person overlooking the tennis courts, its arms raised triumphantly overhead. The town had a ceremony for him the year before he died of that horrible disease. They unveiled the sculpture before a small crowd of mostly students and faculty. Doris was there, and she was startled by the sight of Waylan's famous son. His eyes were deep gray pockets, and gone were the tight brown curls that once peeked beneath the seam of his winter hat. The little hair he had was combed back, straight and shiny. And he was thin. His hands were knobby and pale. He was nearly half her age, yet she was sure he didn't have the strength to lift one of the large ceramic pots she had back at the shop. The world out there had gotten to him; there was barely anything left. He was helped around by a woman with large glasses and a bobbed black wig, and at times he seemed removed from what was going on around him. After the ceremony Owen stood and thanked the crowd. Then he shook his head for a long time. When people began to stir he finally said, "It's so strange to be back here. Like I used to be someone else."

Doris moved closer to the front window. Across the street she could see Isaac Fisher pull his carriage to the curb and climb out favoring his good leg. Isaac sold bees wax candles and organic mushrooms at the farmer's market on North Street, where many of the Amish set up makeshift stands on the weekends. Doris wondered if the news had found him yet, and, in turn, how it weighed on him. She felt the need to apologize, though for what, she wasn't sure. For being part of society and all its ills, perhaps, for resisting a simpler existence. And in that instant she imagined climbing into his carriage and disappearing into the quiet of his world.

When she next looked at the clock it was almost seven, and she went outside and waited a good fifteen minutes for Jon Bishop to open up. She sometimes brought him coffee early in the day, a thank you gesture for shoveling her front walk each winter, and occasionally she'd give him a small bouquet of flowers to display at the counter, some color to brighten up the place. But now she stood empty-handed, working her fingers until she heard him wrestling with the lock. He was freshly shaven and smiling, the scent of Old Spice washing over her as he held open the door. She told him what had happened the night before, not ten feet from where they stood.

"It was boys from outside of town," she said. "No weapons or nothing. Just beat the life clean out of him."

Jon stepped outside and looked up and down the front walk.

"Good lord," he said. "What kind of person could do such a thing?"

What kind of person? She hadn't thought to ask when Ronald was on the phone. All morning she'd been trying to imagine the boy who was killed. Now she wondered about the ones responsible, too, and all of the faces she saw were black faces.

"Unbelievable," Jon said. "These kids running wild like a bunch of animals."

Jon took a hard line when it came to the students. He and Doris had to sweep cigarette butts and coffee cups from the front walk each week, and last homecoming they put a crack in Jon's front window that stretched to the opposite corner in the afternoon sun. But from the stoop of his shoulders she could see he was frightened, like her. For the first time in the entire sixty-three years she had lived there, Doris felt as if Waylan were under attack. She pointed out exactly where it had happened. Someone had already left a handful of wilted asters fanned out on the concrete.

"I suppose I'll go put something together," she said.

Back at the shop Doris locked the door behind her. She sat behind the register and watched the traffic outside, listened to the hum of fluorescent lights. It felt to her like some great and terrible change had occurred, one that everyone in town would someday point to as the start of days more horrible than this. Because what she had always loved about Waylan, what kept her here all these years, was its sameness, that each day came and went so much like the one that had preceded it. Waylan wasn't stricken with the larger evils she read about in the papers, headlines that made her shake her head and whisper a prayer in the exhale. But now those evils were creeping in from Langley and Watertown, maybe as far as Philadelphia, and it left her with the cold realization that one morning she could wake to find Waylan completely unrecognizable. She worried that somehow, when nobody was looking, Waylan might become as volatile as everyplace else. Because things like this didn't happen. Not in Waylan. Not here.

LANGLEY

N OT FIFTEEN MILES north of Waylan was the city of Langley, a sprawling, dried-up industrial town where Joel Martin
lived with his mother and his brother, Derek. Theirs was an end
unit in a stretch of 1950s row houses, a narrow three-bedroom
with long hallways and chalky plaster walls. It was the three of
them and had been for years, living on top of one another in that
cramped, drafty house, which seemed to shrink a little with
each passing day.

A few blocks away was Lindley Street, a short dead-end road
with only a few houses, and that was where Joel and Derek were
now. It was late and they were parked about thirty yards from
the house they were watching. Derek was behind the wheel of
Joel's car, nervously drumming his knees with his fingers.

The house was getting a complete overhaul: new floors, siding, kitchen and bathroom, fresh sod out front. There was a
dumpster in the driveway. Over the past year the housing market had exploded. People were buying places to fix them up and
flip them a few months later, and now everyone wanted in. Many
of the owners lived in Philadelphia and New York, people with
lots of money and no experience in real estate. They hired contractors to do the renovations then turned the place over on the
first bid. In and out. And even with the contractors charging too

much for labor, there were still huge profits to be had. That was how out of hand the market had gotten. There was enough for everyone. Enough, Joel had decided, for him, too.

"You sure it's empty?" Derek said.

"Sure as hell looks it," Joel said.

"Maybe we should wait it out a while. A few more days."

"The lights have been out all week," Joel said. "There's no one in there."

Derek had a weak stomach when it came to trouble, which was exactly why Joel brought him on. He'd been doing these jobs for almost a year now, and though he'd never had any real scrapes there were a few nights that could have easily gone wrong. At the last job in Holt Station Joel came out of a house at two a.m. to find a neighbor unloading groceries from the trunk of his car, and he stood there frozen in the darkness until the guy went inside. Since then he felt the need for an extra set of eyes, and there was no one he could trust more than Derek. He needed someone who was careful, who wouldn't get sloppy after a few jobs, and fear kept you that way.

It didn't take much to get Derek on board. Joel told him the child support was killing him and that they both needed the extra cash if they were ever going to get out of their mother's house and on with their lives, which was all true. But Joel had found something he loved in these jobs. The planning, the power he felt being somewhere he wasn't supposed to be, the high he got afterwards. Breaking the law was something he was good at and he liked being good at something.

Joel reached into the back seat for the pry bar. He didn't like the idea of hitting a place so close to home—someone could recognize the car—but he'd be quick. Contractors weren't always careful about locking up. With any luck one of the windows might be open.

Derek stopped drumming but now his knee was going. "How much longer we gonna sit here?" he said.

Joel popped the car door. "I'll do this alone. It'll be easier."

"You sure?" Derek said.

"I'll have you pull up when I'm ready. Don't move before then."

Derek shifted in his seat. He seemed both relieved and over-whelmed with the responsibility of doing nothing.

"Derek," Joel said. "All right?"

"Yeah. I got it."

THERE WAS ENOUGH light from the streetlamps to make out shapes in the backyard. Joel could see a picnic table by the shed, a garden hose stretched across the lawn; up against the foundation was an old ten-speed. Signs of life. Derek might have been right—someone could still be living here. But it was possible this stuff was left by the last owners, especially if the house sold below asking price. Getting low-balled was something people took personally, and leaving a mess behind was a nice way to flip off the new owners on the way out.

Joel climbed onto the bulkhead and peered inside. He popped open the screen and tried to lift the window, and when it wouldn't budge he covered the glass with a rag and drove the pry bar through. He cleared the remaining glass out of the frame as best he could and draped the rag over the sill. With a deep breath he wormed his way inside.

The house smelled like the inside of an old refrigerator. He'd bet the roof was bad, and there may have been mold issues if water had found its way to the drywall. This was a complete gut-job. From the look of the place Joel could see the contractor was dragging his feet. They were more than a week in and still hadn't gotten past demo.

Joel walked carefully through the house. All of the rooms were empty: no gear, no materials, nothing. He wondered if the crew had been taking everything home, but who would go through the hassle of loading up each night only to unload again the next morning? He checked the bedrooms and opened all the closets. Then he found the basement door and stood at the top of the stairs looking down into the darkness. He had already broken in, already taken the risk. The last thing he wanted was to come away empty-handed.

Upstairs his eyes had adjusted well to the darkness, but in the basement stairwell he could see nothing but blotchy memories of light. He had to use the handrail to get down the steps, and when he reached the bottom a chill skittered across his shoulders. He imagined being filmed from above, under the green haze of an infrared camera. He thought of the people on the other side of that camera, cross-armed cops, judges and D.A.s, his son in Lynn's arms, all of them watching him scramble around in the dark like a scavenger. It was right then that something touched him.

His first thought was that someone had left a dog down there to watch over the place, and now the animal was behind him, teeth bared and ready to strike. He heard a low growl. But at the tail end of that same instant he thought a person had grabbed him. In a panic he spun around, arms stretched, ready to hold off whatever was there. It didn't take a full second for all this to happen, or for him to recognize his cell phone vibrating in his pocket. Derek.

"The fuck you calling me for?" he said.

"What's going on? You're taking forever."

"Stay where you are. I'll tell you when—"

He lifted his eyes to a band of soft blue light spilling from the screen of his phone. He could see clear to the other end of the basement, past the stairs and to the opposite corner by the bulkhead. It was all there, stacked neatly on an old moving blanket.

"Jesus Christ," he said. "Pull up. I'm coming out."

DELL LIVED in the sticks outside of Hempstead. It was mostly bare land out there, overgrown and unfarmed, a few rundown houses dotting the landscape. Joel hated even passing through. Being in the country made him uneasy. There was too much open space and not enough eyes to keep everyone in check, because only the worst kind of trouble happened when there was no one around to see it. Even the roughest city streets had people, witnesses, but out here it seemed lawless. A guy at work named Bowers once told him about the time he took a bullet in his quarter panel while driving out past Lancaster. It was broad daylight and the shots came from somewhere at the edge of the woods, he'd said, and no one, "not one goddamn soul," saw it happen. Later, when Bowers reported it to the police, the officer took his statement with a deadpan that said no one would follow up, because what was there to follow up on? The story only proved what Joel already knew, that being out in the sticks was dangerous, especially when you were dealing with people like Dell. Hell, there could be shallow graves not twenty yards from the road he was on now and no one would ever know any different.

Derek was staring out the passenger-side window. He hadn't said much since Joel had shaken him awake earlier that morning. He had a cigarette going, one of Joel's, a bad sign already. The job last night might have been too much for him. He was too sensitive was his problem. He thought too much about what things meant. When they were kids Joel sometimes let him sleep on his bedroom floor. It started in the weeks after their father disappeared, and there, coiled up in blankets alongside Joel's bed, Derek would release all his fears into the darkness. He'd tell Joel how scared he was not having their dad in the house, how someone could break in and their mom wouldn't be able to fight the guy off. He worried that they might never see their dad again, that they'd have to move far away from their home. Joel would wait until Derek got it all out. That was the best he could do for his brother, to listen and hope it might set him at ease long enough for them to get some rest.

Joel snatched his cigarettes off Derek's lap. "Jesus, wake up already."

Derek handed him the lighter. "Yeah," he said.

"You should have stayed home. I told you I don't need you for this."

Derek brought up something from the back of his throat and spit it out the window.

"This whole thing," he said. "It doesn't sit right."

"What did you think it was going to be like? It'll be fine. We're careful."

"It's not that," Derek said. "We're stealing from working guys. Guys like us."

"Most of them have insurance. They'll get their money back."

"It's their livelihood, man. How are they gonna work without gear?"

Joel fought the urge to pull hard to the shoulder and slam on the breaks.

"You knew all this going in. We went through this a million times."

"I know, I know. I'm just saying."

"What?" Joel said. "What are you saying?"

Derek would be fine once he got past this part. Joel had learned long ago that all Derek really needed in moments like this was time to settle in. Pretty soon all the noise in his head would fade and he'd realize the world wasn't half as scary as he'd made it out to be. It wasn't his fault. This was how he was wired. Joel would have to be patient.

"Forget it," Derek said.

They took the rest of the ride in silence, speeding through the long, twisting roads. Joel was moving pretty good. He'd bought the car from a drywaller he'd met on a work site in Hollis. It was a '98 Impala with 105,000 miles. The guys he worked with said he looked like a state trooper tooling around in the thing, but the car had balls. He took the curves with as much speed as he could handle, opening it up when the road straightened. With his eyes locked on the road he flew by Dell's street and had to circle back. The house sat at the top of the hill. He could see Dell sitting on the front porch as they pulled up the gravel driveway.

Derek was out of the car before Joel had it in park. He slammed the passenger door behind him, but Joel didn't think it meant anything. This was a new situation and Derek didn't want to look soft. He was a tough kid when he needed to be, fierce if you got him to that point, and here he was only asserting that.

Joel headed to the house with Derek lagging a few paces behind, and when he got to the stairs he was startled back a step. Dell laughed from his chest, wheezing until it sent him into a coughing fit.

"What the hell is that?" Joel said.

"They're pigs," Dell said. "Vietnamese Potbellies. I just got 'em."

"What are they for?" Derek said, and Dell turned as if he'd right then noticed Joel wasn't alone.

"They're pets," he said to Derek. "For fun. A friend of mine sells them on the internet. He gave me a deal."

"Why didn't you just get a dog?" Joel said.

"These things are smarter than dogs. You can train 'em and everything."

Joel took a knee and one of the pigs started sniffing around his legs. It was small, about the size of a puppy. The hair on its body was black and stiff like the bristles of a hairbrush. He ran a hand down its back and the pig swung around and snapped at his fingers.

"That one's Sadie," Dell said, scratching at the side of his head. "She's not very sweet."

Joel stood to try to move things along. "The trunk is full. Where do you want this stuff?"

Dell was facing Derek now, looking him over as if they'd met before and Dell was trying to remember where. He got strangely close.

"Who's this?" he said, scanning Derek's face.

"That's my brother. He's been giving me a hand."

Dell was slack-jawed. "Brother, huh? I don't see much resemblance."

The two were locked on one another. Joel could see Derek getting impatient.

"You look familiar," Dell said. "Ever been to the O.T.B.?"

Derek glanced over at Joel. "No. Never."

"How about the diner out in Warren Creek? There's a Greek fella owns the place. Bolovenos. I ran numbers with his son a few years back. Kinda got your jawline."

"Dell, we need to be somewhere," Joel said. "Why don't you come take a look."

"Because I thought I knew who I was doing business with. Now all of a sudden I'm staring at a brother that bears not one goddamn resemblance to you. That's the hell why."

"He's my brother, okay. Check his I.D. if you don't believe us. Jesus, stop being so paranoid."

"I make my living being paranoid. What do you need help for, anyway?"

"So there are no surprises. You're the one always telling me to be careful."

Dell chewed on the idea and faced Derek again. "Well, if you're gonna be on board with me there's some things you'll need to understand."

"I explained everything already," Joel said. "He's heard it."

"Then he can hear it again, goddamn it. You'll need to keep your mouth shut. Period. You hear what I'm saying? If the cops come up on you, you let it happen until we can deal with it later. I'm a ghost as far as you're concerned."

"I get it," Derek said.

"Be sure that you do."

"He understands," Joel said. "Can we get on with this?"

Dell chewed at the air for a while. "You sure you're not a Bolovenos?"

Derek shook his head. "Man, you're thinking of someone else."

Dell looked relieved. "He was a son of a bitch, that one. Didn't like to pay. His old man makes good burgers, though, if you're out that way." He clapped his hands. "All right, then, let's see what you boys have for me." He made his way to the car with Sadie nosing after his footsteps.

"Where the hell did you find this guy?" Derek said.

From behind Dell looked like nothing more than an old man breaking down a little at a time. But Joel tried not to think of him that way. From the beginning he sensed what Dell might be capable of, and he made it a point to never let his guard down. They'd met at The Windsock, out by the airport, a dive that mostly served old men. Joel liked to go there when he was in the mood to drink hard. There was no jukebox or people his age; the television flashed soundlessly in the corner. It was a place to get loaded without distraction. And one night when Joel was on his third shot of Jack Daniel's, Dell came over and pulled up a chair.

"My name is Delano Wilkes," he said, tapping the AJ Construction logo on Joel's shirt pocket, "and I been looking for someone like you."

When everything was out of the trunk Joel followed Dell and Sadie into the house. The pig that had remained on the porch was gone, but Dell didn't seem concerned.

Dell's place wasn't bad, but there wasn't much in the way of furniture. The living room had a drab green couch and a couple of end tables; in the corner by the window was a straight-backed wooden chair that didn't seem at all comfortable. Joel spotted what could only be a high school graduation picture on the mantle. It was a girl with big hair and bright green eyes that matched her satin blouse. He could see some of Dell in the girl's face: the sharp corners of her mouth, the wide eyebrows. She was pretty but the picture was old.

"Making yourself at home?" Dell said.

He held up the picture. "This your daughter, Dell?"

"Yeah it's my daughter. Why?"

"You never said you had a daughter."

"Why should I? It's none of your business about her."

Joel set the picture back on the mantle. "I don't know. I thought maybe I'd give her a call. Get to know her a little."

"Okay, smartass. I'll give you eight hundred for the lot." He slapped the wad of cash onto the end table.

"Are you kidding? It's worth three times that. There's a nail gun with a compressor. That miter saw has a laser."

"I still have to move it. I suppose I could go as high as a grand." He pulled a few more bills from his pocket. "Where else you gonna get cash this quick?"

"For chrissake," Joel said. He snatched the money off the table and pointed it at Dell. "Don't think I'm happy about this."

"Well, if you boys are looking for extra money I have other jobs than this sort of thing."

Joel moved to the window and started counting, laying fifties on the sill so Dell would know how careful he was, how he couldn't be cheated.

"That sound like something you might be interested in?"

Joel could see Derek sitting in the car. He'd swiped another cigarette and the smoke was rippling out the open window. His eyes were shut and he had his head back against the headrest, wondering, no doubt, what was next.

JOEL HAD PROMISED Lynn he'd be at her place by noon, but that wasn't going to happen. Dell had taken longer than he figured, and by the time he dropped Derek off at home it was already close to one o'clock. When he finally got there Lynn opened the door little more than a crack so he could let himself in the rest of the way. He entered to find Sam on all fours, raking through a pile of Legos that were scattered on the carpet.

Sam was a different kid every time Joel saw him. By his first birthday, his eyes had changed from an icy gray to brown; his hair, straight and dark like Joel's early on, had begun to curl. Now he was showing Lynn's heavy bottom lip, her round face. Joel was finding less of himself in the boy all the time.

Sam jumped to his feet and Joel scooped him up by the waist and lifted him high into the air. He laid him out on the carpet and went for the ribs until Sam started laughing too hard to make a sound.

Joel was able to get over there about once a week, which probably wasn't enough. But Sam was always in his head. At night, he fantasized about watching over his son, rescuing him. It was always the same scene, one he never tired of. The two of them are at the park. Sam climbs the jungle gym and hangs straight-armed from the bars, his feet dangling only an inch or two from the ground. But then Joel becomes distracted and when he turns back Sam is gone, led away by someone tall and faceless in a gray hoodie. Joel spots the guy taking Sam by the hand, walking him towards a nearby parking lot, and then he pulls Sam under his arm and begins to run. It never takes Joel long to catch them, and when he does he grips the guy's windpipe so hard Joel can feel his fists tightening in bed. Most nights he could run through the ending two or three times before drifting off. He never told anyone he did this. He was afraid people would think he was some sick fuck for imagining his own son in harm's way, because, if it were someone else, that was exactly what he'd think.

Sam put up his fists.

"Higher," Joel said. "You have to protect your face." He threw a few slow jabs so Sam could block them.

Sam reared back and held the position as if he were about to deliver a knockout blow and wanted to showboat for the crowd.

"Come and get it mo-fo."

"Hey," Lynn said. She took Sam by the arm and pulled him close. "Watch that mouth. Understand? I don't want to hear that kind of talk."

Sam buried his face in her thigh.

"Real nice," she said to Joel.

"What? That's not from me."

"I'm sure. And laughing doesn't help."

"He doesn't even know what it means."

"That's not the point. You get him all wound up."

She put a hand on Sam's forehead and felt his ears, which were pink and shiny. "You need to settle down. Why don't you show Daddy your Lego set. I have to run downstairs."

Sam hitched up his pants from the back and kneeled. "Come on, Daddy," he said.

Lynn left with a full laundry basket and Joel stretched out on the floor. He turned the empty Lego box in his hands. It was a large set with a rocket ship theme, one of the more expensive ones from the size of it.

"Who got you this?" he said.

"Grandma June," Sam said.

"What for?"

Sam shrugged.

"You must have been pretty good to get a toy for no reason."

"I'm really good," he said. "All the time."

Joel watched Sam slip his fingernail between the seam of two blocks and try to work them apart. He hated not knowing what was going on in his son's life, and it seemed to be happening more often these days. When he and Lynn first split she would call with weekly updates to let him know the smallest details:

visits to her brother's house in Philly, play dates with other kids. But eventually the calls tapered off and now it was like he was being left out of the conversation entirely.

Joel picked through the blocks—bright reds and yellows and blues, a few clear axels and a ninety degree hinge. He found a pair of matching girders to use as a frame and added cylinders to the back like rocket boosters. Deep in the pile he found red triangle wings and a small windshield for the cockpit, and behind it he put one of the yellow Lego men that came with the set.

"Check it out." He moved the ship through the air and made laser sounds.

Sam snatched it out of his hand.

"Hey," Joel said. "Don't grab that from me."

"No," Sam said. "Not like that. Watch me do it." He began pulling the ship apart one piece at a time.

"'Watch me do it,'" Joel whined. "'Watch me do it.' How am I supposed to play with you if I can't touch the pieces?"

"What's going on?" Lynn said. She dropped the empty laundry basket in the corner.

"He won't let me touch his stuff. Will you?" He tugged at Sam's ear until the boy swatted him away.

"Don't tease him," Lynn said.

"I'm trying to play with him. All he wants is for me to watch."

"Enough, all right."

To Sam, she said, "Why don't you go play in your room for a few minutes. I want to talk to Daddy."

"I don't want to," Sam said.

"It'll only be a few minutes. Then you two can play some more. Go."

The boy darted from the room. When he was out of sight Lynn went into the kitchen. She returned with a fresh glass of iced tea for herself and took a seat on the couch. Her hair was shorter than the last time he'd seen her, but only a little. She had gradually been going shorter ever since Sam was born, never more than an inch or so, nothing drastic, only enough to change her look over long stretches of time, a look that was becoming increasingly professional. He imagined taking her in his hands, but the thought quickly left him. A long time ago he'd reached a point where any closeness to her—her kiss, her scent—made something roil inside him. Toward the end, when they were still trying to make it work, he had to fight the urge to recoil from her touch. But there were still times he wanted to fuck her, without affection, without love. Just fuck until the two of them were spent. Sometimes she would slip into his fantasies uninvited, always in the last moments, and she still excited him enough to put him over the top.

Joel took a seat in the wicker chair beside the TV, which made splintering noises as he settled in. He put a stack of bills on the coffee table.

"For the month," he said.

Lynn scooped up the money and tapped it against the glass tabletop, watching him as if she somehow knew where it had come from.

"Hey, why'd your mother buy him that Lego set?"

"She didn't. It's a hand-me-down."

"From who?"

She huffed. "Lisa from work. Why does it matter?"

"It doesn't. Can't I ask a freakin' question?"

Lynn chewed at the inside of her cheek. She looked at the floor and back at him, and then she dropped the money onto the table and swallowed hard.

"We're moving," she said.

Joel waited out the silence.

"Brian's retiring soon and his daughter is taking over the practice. She wants to move down to Florida. Sometime next year. They're offering me a raise, plus moving expenses."

Everything she said sounded rehearsed, as if she had practiced in front of the bathroom mirror.

"That's crazy. What are you going to move all the way down there for?"

"It's a good opportunity. There's nothing crazy about it."

Lynn had been a paralegal for a few years now. He'd thought it was a dumb idea when she first started going to school, but only because he couldn't imagine her in that kind of environment, suits and lawyers, rich douchebags like the people he did jobs for in Bethlehem. She laced her fingers, watching him with a patience he found unnerving.

"So you're leaving? You weren't even going to talk to me about it?"

"Joel."

"How am I supposed to see my son?"

"You barely see him now," she said, then appeared sorry for it. "We have a year to work all that out. The schools down there are good. We can get out of this shitty apartment."

"Come on. Can't you find a job around here?"

"It's not that," Lynn said. "It would be a fresh start. It feels right."

"It sounds fucking crazy to me."

"I'm not asking your permission. We're going and there's nothing you can do." Then, more gently, she said, "This is a good thing. For Sam, too."

Joel slumped in the chair as if he planned to sit there until she changed her mind. "Does he know?"

"He's excited about the beaches. Says he wants to look for buried treasure." She tried to force a smile. "It may not be for good. I want to at least give it a year, see how it goes. That's not long."

Joel thought back to what he was doing a year ago. As far as he could remember, nothing in his life was different.

"A year," he said. "And then what?"

Lynn folded her arms, shrugged. "Then we see."

ARLENE KNEW her drawer would be off. Sometimes she could feel it, a slight, nagging angle of gravity pulling at her as if her own carelessness had tipped the world off balance. It was only ten dollars. An even ten; how could she have missed that? Now she had to wait for Rachel Starks, the branch manager, to come sign off on the mistake so they could go home for the night. Arlene turned her hands in the sunlight pouring through the front window. They were a mess, ashy and raw from washing them too often with antibacterial soap; the tips of her fingers had painful splits that extended beneath the nail.

Arlene had worked at the Citizens Bank for nineteen years, had been head-teller for fifteen, and in that time the job, much like the money she handled, had changed. There was a time when customers were pleasant, but no more, not even on nice days. They approached the window with suspicion, braced themselves for confrontation. And if there were a problem, some small issue that needed to be dealt with, they took it personally. The younger people asked to speak with a manager, as if Arlene were neither important nor intelligent enough to deal with the situation. Then they twisted her words, trying to portray themselves as victims of her misdirection rather than what they were: people bent on getting around the rules.

The seniors were no better. They acted as if their money alone were keeping the institution solvent (even if they didn't have any money), and for that they expected special treatment. They huffed and wagged their heads if they had to wait in line, and when they were told they had to follow procedure, like everyone else, they threw up their hands and announced, loud enough for everyone to hear, that after all these years the Citizens Bank had "gone downhill."

Worse was what was going on out on the floor. The managers were pushing big loans these days, much bigger than people could handle. Couples in their 30s were getting pre-approved for $300,000 mortgages. How could they afford it? It seemed to Arlene that people were living beyond their means, and it was only a matter of time before something happened, something big enough to affect not only the irresponsible but everyone with money in the bank.

And now the money itself was different. The face on the bills was large and off-center; there was no longer any symmetry. The change in design was meant to make it easier to spot counterfeits, but for Arlene it did exactly the opposite. All bills looked phony to her now. These new bills were as coarse as fine-grit sandpaper and left a gray film on her hands that irritated her skin, which compelled her to leave her station several times a day to wash.

Rachel appeared beside her and dropped a large ring of keys onto the counter.

"How much?" she said.

"Ten dollars. I'm sorry."

Rachel flipped open the first compartment and pulled a thin stack of fifties from the drawer.

"Maybe it's the breaks you've been taking. I've seen you, Arlene. Those little interruptions can be a distraction."

"I'm only gone a minute or two. Never when it's busy."

"We're all gears that fit into one another. Take one out and everything stops. Do you understand what I'm saying?"

Arlene did not. Whenever she left to wash her hands everything went on without her. The world kept moving. As head teller, Arlene only worked the window at the busiest times of the day, so customers never noticed when she was gone. What did it matter? Washing her hands was a compulsion, sure, but a harmless one. And it gave her a chance to think, about her boys, about Joel. Lately, she'd been worried. He was quieter than usual, always in a rush. Something was going on, and she was afraid that he'd managed to involve Derek in whatever it was. They'd been spending time together, heading out at night and early in the morning, riding in the same car. They traded glances, subtle nods, communicating in a way far too intimate for the brothers they were. She had tried several times to talk to him, but Joel could always convince her things were fine, even when deep down she knew otherwise. It was like that with him. A first child has a way of stealing your better judgment.

"I guess I've been preoccupied," she said. Then she added, "My son."

Rachel stopped counting and turned to face her. She was a tall, broad-shouldered woman with a heavy gaze, and her attempts at compassion were often intimidating.

"These kids will be our undoing, won't they?" she said, and started over.

Later that evening Arlene sat in her kitchen listening to the radio. She heard the sick rumble of Joel's car coming up the driveway, the suck of weather stripping as he opened the front door. He lingered in the hall, stomping the dirt from his boots.

When he stopped, she called, "You hungry?"

There was no response, and right when she figured he might ignore her and head upstairs he said, "Any coffee?"

"There's some left," she said. "Come sit down."

He entered the kitchen with a washed-out look of jetlag, in need of a meal and solid hours of sleep. As she filled one of the large mugs he dropped into the chair, more out of frustration, it seemed, than exhaustion. He played with the hair at the back of his head, twisting the strands between his fingers. He had done this since he was a child, watching television or doing his homework, any time he was trying to shut out life's distractions so he could concentrate. Such a strange habit, especially for a boy like Joel.

"You see your brother?" she said.

"Not since this morning," he said, picking at his fingernail. Then, perhaps sensing she was watching, he looked at her. "Lynn's moving to Florida."

Arlene took the chair next to him. "What are you talking about?"

"Just what I said. Her office is gonna move next year. She wants to go with them. That's all. Sayonara."

"Florida? How can she go all the way down there? She won't know anyone. What about Sam?"

Joel clucked his tongue, fidgeting as if he knew the exact words she was going to say.

"I mean, did she consider you at all? A boy shouldn't be separated from his father like that."

"Stop," he said.

"But it's not right, Joel. Doesn't she know what it can do to Sam, not having you around? That boy thinks you hung the moon. This isn't something to take lightly."

"You think I don't know that?" He rubbed the back of his neck. "There's nothing I can do about it. I can't make her stay. If she wants to go she can go. Fuck it."

She could hear Joel's phone buzzing in his pocket, but he didn't make a move to answer it.

He shook his head and put up his hands as if he were surrendering. "So what do I do, then?"

"Maybe you can talk it through with her. After you've settled down. She might be willing to change her mind."

He watched her a moment and nodded. "Okay," he said, and went for his phone.

She expected him to take the call into the other room, but instead he stretched back in the chair and crossed his legs at the ankles. He looked so rundown for a young man. His eyes were red-rimmed and heavy, as though he'd been up half the night wrestling with regret. He'd always been the handsome one of her boys—much more so than Derek, who'd been red-faced and doughy since the day he was born—but now his looks were beginning to harden. His ratty stubble, that broken front tooth of his. He had chipped it during a game of touch football years ago. Only the corner of his tooth was broken. The break wasn't even high enough to catch the nerve. But Joel stood before the bathroom mirror for hours, running his tongue over the jagged edge until the flesh was red and tender. He wanted to have the tooth repaired, but Arlene told him he was making too much of it. She remembered taking him by the chin and moving his head from side to side. She told him crowns were yellow and bulky and didn't sit right in people's mouths. Besides, she wasn't about to pay a dentist to fix what didn't hurt.

"It's fine," she had told him. "You can barely see it."

But now, work-worn and unshaven in the light of her kitchen all these years later, that tooth made him appear so menacing, a person to avoid on the street.

Joel moved into the living room. She could hear him saying something about a park as he headed upstairs. So much of him was hidden from her, and if Lynn moved away she worried that Joel might vanish from her life entirely. That little boy was all that kept him grounded, it seemed. Take Sam away and who knew where he might end up.

But the longer she sat with the idea, the more she understood that Lynn was only trying to do right by Sam. Joel was no kind of father. He didn't understand the need for discipline and guidance, for setting an example. He loved his son and thought that was enough, but love was only the start of a long list of what that boy needed, and Joel didn't have it in him to provide the rest. Lynn was only trying to create some distance before he could do any real damage, and the longer she waited, the worse it would get. Arlene certainly knew. She'd made that mistake herself.

Rachel (boss of bank)

Arlene

Dell (sketchy friend)

Derek Joel Lynn

Sam

BROTHERS

O N THE DAY he was killed Christopher Roche wasn't in love,
but he was something close to that. He'd only been in Waylan a few months and it all felt new to him, the town, his routine,
the people around him; every day seemed to hold the promise of
a more interesting life. His parents were surprised he'd chosen
Waylan University, where his brother Rich was finishing a degree in Anthropology five years after he'd begun. With Christopher's grades they thought he'd leave Pennsylvania for a bigger
world, but Christopher felt at home in Waylan ever since they
first moved Rich into the freshman dorms, back when Christopher was still in middle school. The town was like being in a
painting from centuries ago, a small island of civilization in a
sea of farmland, quiet and manageable and removed from the
strip malls and wide three-lane thoroughfares of his hometown.
Waylan had no facades, no pretenses.

He had grown up in Kings Row, about twenty miles outside
Philly, a place, Christopher felt, where people prepared for what
was next rather than lived, never taking their eyes off the horizon of college, career, that next promotion, retirement, never
appreciating where they were at the moment. Most of his friends
were running down the summer at home, same as last year,
working at the outlet mall or the new Wegmans, life-guarding

at the community pool, saving their money for the fall semester. Always preparing. At night they went to the movies and coalesced at the Starlight Diner. Christopher had tired of the routine long ago, and he moved to Waylan a few weeks early so he could instead take in the town slowly. The plan was to stay at Rich's place for a while, then, once the semester started, move into the dorms, which were right up the road.

He liked to think that, in their way, he and Rich were close. His most vivid memories of his brother were when they were small, playing in the woods the day after that huge blizzard in '97, or the night they lay side-by-side on the back lawn during the summer blackout, silent and awestruck by a sky that held more stars than they'd ever thought existed. But once Rich hit his teens the nearly six years between them put him on the periphery of Christopher's life. By the time Rich entered high school he spent most of his time in his room with the door closed, listening to Radiohead albums, fiddling with the bass guitar he'd gotten for Christmas. On weekends he spent nights at his buddy Tyler's house, jamming with the band they'd pieced together with a few other kids from school, a "pseudo-rock/punk/fusion amalgamation" called It's Pronounced Nuclear. Christopher hadn't heard them play because their sound never made it past the confines of Tyler's basement, but also because that part of Rich's life was off limits, as if Christopher, who was still in grammar school, didn't have a place there.

But there was excitement in Rich's voice when Christopher first called to say he was coming to Waylan, and it was Rich who suggested he come out early. His parents drove him to town in the new Explorer on a sweltering July afternoon, AC blasting, his mother gazing pensively out the window the entire ride. When the three of them stepped from the car Rich went straight to Christopher, shook his hand and pulled him in for a half-hug, something he'd never done before.

"You finally made it," he said, which Christopher took to mean more than the ride up.

His father hitched up his shorts as he took in Rich's latest place, a small ranch sandwiched between two sections of row houses, the entire block a weathered strip of neglected student housing. There were tufts of tall, spiny weeds growing out of cracks in the front walk; bright green moss covered the shaded half of the roof.

"So this is where my eight hundred a month is going," his father said.

Rich shrugged him off. "It's not so bad. Has a nice rustic quality, no?"

His father jangled the keys in his pocket. "Quite the racket they got out here. We should have invested in this town years ago, Sheila. We're missing out on a goldmine."

"Shush," his mother said and went to Rich for a hug. She closed her eyes and squeezed tight, then pulled back to have a look at him. He had a full beard now, which had come in lighter than his hair. "What's all this?"

Rich pulled his beard to a point at the chin. "Been trying it out. What do you think?" He turned to show off his profile.

"I'll need some time with it," she said and touched his face. "Here, this is for you." She held up a large shopping bag. Inside were rolls of toilet paper and coffee, laundry detergent and deodorant and toothpaste. "I should have picked up some razors, I guess."

"Any food in there?"

She nodded. "There's a tray of lasagna on the bottom. I'm afraid your brother got into it before I could stop him."

"It was in the fridge," Christopher said. "How could I know?"

His mother leaned her head to the side. "I'm already getting used to the beard. You look like your Uncle Robbie, you know that? Doesn't he, Peter?"

His father was standing beneath a dogwood tree that leaned precariously toward the house. He looked up into the canopy and pushed against the crooked trunk.

Later that evening, after their parents said their goodbyes—their father hugging Christopher tight, patting him hard on the back, offering only a handshake to Rich—he and Rich drank beer on the back porch and listened to the distant rush of cars on the turnpike. They finished a roach Rich had left over from the night before. Rich came out of the house with two more beers and handed one to Christopher.

"You shoulda seen my last place. We were in the sticks out in Hempstead. Whole lotta nothing out there. Had some great parties, though. No one ever bothered us."

Christopher cracked open his beer and shook the foam from his fingers. "Landlord throw you out?"

"No, we left. It was too isolated. It got pitch black at night, no streetlights or anything. And the house was creepy as fuck. Had these really low ceilings that made you feel boxed in. This one night Glen heard someone moaning out in the woods. Dragged my ass out of bed at like two in the morning because he couldn't sleep. But I heard it, too. It was weird. I couldn't tell if it was an animal or a person. He thought someone was calling for help, but I didn't hear that. But that sound, man. Like when a cat's in heat. Scared the hell out of us."

Christopher felt tremors of laughter rumbling in his gut, probably from the weed.

"Turned out it was some old lady," Rich said. "Her house was miles away." Rich pointed to the opposite end of the lawn as if the house could be seen from where they sat. "I guess she fell and hurt herself. She was there for a while, I heard. Hours." He leaned his head back against the railing as if the story were over.

"So, what happened?"

"Nothing happened," he said. "It stopped after a while. I went back to bed."

"You didn't do anything?"

"It was two o'clock in the morning. We didn't know if someone was screwing around or what."

"She needed your help, man. Why didn't you call the cops?"

"And say what? Glen thought it was a ghost." He tugged at his beard a moment. "I guess we should have. It was pretty far away. Sound travels in the woods. You'd be surprised. I heard she was okay, though."

Christopher pried the tab from his beer and flicked it into the recycling bin beside the steps. The story had gotten under his skin. He felt like he was being watched.

"We ought to hike through Blue Rock," Rich said. "There are some nice trails up there. I saw a black bear once."

They stayed up close to dawn, and when Rich passed out on the couch Christopher went outside to have a cigarette. His parents didn't like the idea of him coming out so soon. They had hoped he might spend the entire summer at home, right down to the last possible day, so he could spend time with his friends, with his girlfriend, Michele, enjoy this last stretch of youth. But somewhere in his senior year of high school Christopher had become restless. He'd grown tired of his parents' constant focus. His father had attended every one of his swim meets, oftentimes leaving work early for the afternoon competitions. He sat high in the bleachers and marked his times whether they were good or not. This was for posterity—like videotaping a child's first steps—as if he didn't want to miss such an important moment, no matter how unimpressive that moment might be.

His mother started doing the legwork for colleges in his freshman year of high school, a time when Christopher could focus on little more than first-person computer games and old sci-fi movies. That same year, while visiting his relatives in Connecticut, she brought him to New Haven so he could see the tall iron gates and gothic architecture of Yale. He had no chance of getting into such a place and would never apply. They both knew that. The excursion was instead meant to introduce him to opportunity, show him the grandness of privilege so he'd perhaps aspire to some slightly lesser greatness himself. He dragged his feet the whole day under a muggy summer haze while his mother soaked everything in. She and his father had both gone to state schools themselves, and he could see her dreaming of other, more grandiose possibilities. As they walked she said, "It's overwhelming, isn't it? There's so much here."

Sometimes her attention built such pressure in his chest he found it difficult to make eye contact. He was grateful for her support. He was. But at times his life, it seemed, belonged not to him but to her, and he couldn't help but resent her for that. When he told her he'd made the decision to attend Waylan she wasn't angry, but there was disappointment, as if he were passing up better options. She sometimes turned away when he told people about his plans. But the way she said goodbye earlier that day had surprised him. Before getting into the car she had Rich and him stand by the front bushes for a picture. Rich put an arm over Christopher's shoulder and grinned while she struggled with her phone.

Then she studied the picture a moment, and as if to give her blessing, she said, "It's good to know my boys are together."

She hopped into the car and fastened the seatbelt, and as they slowly pulled away she leaned out the open window and blew a kiss.

"Look out for each other," she said, though she was looking at Rich.

Christopher flicked his cigarette onto the lawn and leaned back on his elbows. As the sky brightened he felt the anticipation of setting up for a party, from packing a suitcase for vacation. His mind buzzed with what was ahead. It would stay with him, this feeling, right to the end.

Parents

(girlfriend)

Michelle — Christopher   Rich

VISITS

FOR THE THIRD TIME in a little more than a month, Joel's father asked him to swing by to help with the kitchen drain. Joel hated going there now that Charlotte was gone. The last time he visited his father cried in front of him, and sometimes he'd ramble on about how he should've been the one to go first. Talk like that made Joel want to cover his eyes and disappear, especially when it came from his father, who'd never been one to show that side of himself before Charlotte got sick. It was like his sharpest edges had been ground smooth over the last couple of years, and what was left was someone angry and vulnerable and terrified all at once.

When he arrived his father was sitting in front of the television watching a cable news station. The house smelled like an old dive bar. His father had quit smoking when Charlotte was diagnosed with lymphoma over a year ago because she had asked him to, but the place was never going to lose that smell. He'd have to pull up the carpets and paint the walls and replace all the furniture, and even then it would be a house where a smoker used to live. Though he never said so, Joel wished his dad would break down and start smoking again so he might be a little less miserable. Why torture himself now that Charlotte was gone? Of all the promises to keep, his father had chosen one that didn't matter.

His father sat up in the recliner. "Where's Derek?" he said.

"It's a clogged drain. What do I need him for?"

His father winced as he got to his feet and led him to the kitchen. His gout had been bothering him for weeks now, and watching him hobble around was like looking into the future. He wasn't even sixty and already his body was shutting down on him.

"The damn thing won't stay clear," his father said. "I used the plunger but all it does is pack it down more." He grabbed a glass from the draining board and poured himself some whiskey.

"It needs to be snaked out. I keep telling you that."

"The Puerto Rican guy next door tried to give me a hand but I think he made it worse. I shoulda never let him touch it."

The sink was half-full with murky water. Joel worked the plunger for a while, churning up swirling black chunks of muck. He opened the cabinets to get at the pipes below. In the way were detergents and plastic bags and folded dish towels.

"You could have moved this stuff before I came," he said.

"I'll do it now."

"I got it," Joel said.

His father grumbled something and hobbled back to the television. Joel cleared out the cabinet and removed the trap and drained the sink into a bucket. Earlier that week he'd borrowed a small hand-snake from Charlie at work, and he fed it down the pipe until he felt the block. He hated sparring with his old man, but something about being in this house always knotted up his stomach. The weekends he and Derek spent here as kids were like staying with strangers. There was nothing to do. They weren't allowed to go into the refrigerator without asking, and if he and Derek played even a little rough on the living room floor Charlotte would holler as if it were a real fight. Then his father would storm in and give them hell, too. From the moment he'd walk into that house Joel would get antsy, and all these years later the place still had that same hold on him.

It took him close to an hour to finally break through the clog. He put everything back into the cabinet and ran the hot water for a while to try to flush away what was left. After that he went into the living room and fell into the sofa.

"It's better, but you're still going to have to get a plumber. You should get it done so you don't have to worry about it."

His father was watching a square-jawed newscaster go down a list of talking points that appeared on the screen.

"Goddamn pensions," his father mumbled. "It's going to kill guys like us, you know. You watch. When everyone starts cashing in and there isn't enough money left, we're the ones who are going to suffer. You wait and see."

Joel hated when his dad talked about anything in the news. He liked to repeat what he heard on television and on talk radio, sometimes word for word, like the guys Joel worked with. Joel had to listen to the same shit over and over, that the government was trying to tax the working guy to death, that lowlifes and immigrants got handouts on their dime, that the pussies in Congress were holding us back in Iraq. End of the world kind of shit. Joel didn't know what was true and what wasn't, but he couldn't take any of them seriously. He knew every gripe was nothing more than a way of bitching about what was wrong in their own lives.

If he stayed long enough his father would start going on about how everything was better before. To his dad, every bad thing that happened in the world meant they were one step closer to the end, and it was all because people had decided to fix what wasn't broken. The way he told it, you'd think life was perfect back when he was young, and that since then people had lost their way, fooled by dirty politicians and bad teachers and their own stupidity, which brought the world to the mess it was now. But Joel knew that deep down his father wanted the worst to happen, so he could go to his grave with the satisfaction of having seen what the rest of the world had missed.

"How's your boy doing?" his father said.

"He's fine. Getting big." He didn't have the energy to bring up Lynn's plans.

"I was thinking, maybe you could bring him by one day. For the afternoon. I'd like to see him."

"Maybe one Sunday when I have him."

His father looked at him with dead eyes as if he knew this wouldn't happen. His face was slack and deflated.

"I'm his granddad, son. It's only right you bring him by every now and then. He ought to know me while I'm still around."

Joel couldn't see the point. Why get Sam attached only to have his father check out later on? When his father left years ago it was like he blocked Joel and Derek right out of his mind. And it was *how* he left, disappearing without a word then trying to pick up like it had never happened. No point in working Sam over like that, too.

"I been busy, that's all. I'll bring him by when I can."

The muscles in his dad's jaw twitched all the way to the temples. His eyes welled a little. "I miss her, Joel."

"Dad."

"I know," he said. "I know you don't want to hear it. I don't blame you. I don't know what I'm supposed to do. I go to work and I come home and there's nothing else. What's the point of getting out of bed? It's like I'm waiting out the rest of my life."

His father tipped back the rest of his whiskey. "She cared about you boys a lot, you know. She really did."

His father had said this before, but the truth was Joel and Charlotte never really got along. As a kid he ignored her, pretending not to hear when she spoke, avoiding eye contact. Sometimes he'd walk away from her mid-sentence. His father never stepped in, and if Charlotte threw up her arms in frustration his father would pat the air.

"Leave it be, Charlotte," he'd say, and she'd sulk out of the room.

Joel eased up as he got older. They'd say hello and he would even be nice sometimes, but he would also go entire visits without ever saying a word to her, and by then Charlotte had learned to navigate around him. Instead of talking directly to him she'd go through his father.

"Maybe Joel would like something to drink," she'd say, or "Did you tell Joel who we saw last week?"

It was a solution that worked for them.

"I don't know, maybe I should join her," his father said. "At least we'd be together."

Joel shifted in his seat. His dad liked to say this kind of stuff for attention, for sympathy. Joel sometimes had the urge to call him on it, tell him to quit talking and go ahead and off himself, just to see his father's reaction.

"Have another drink and get some sleep," Joel said. "You'll feel better tomorrow."

"Don't end up alone, Joel. If you take anything from me, take that. There's nothing worse in life." His eyes went back to the television.

Joel stood at the opportunity to leave.

"Where you going?"

"I need to get home."

"Already?" his father said. "Why don't you grab a beer. Sit for a minute."

"I got shit to do. I haven't even eaten yet."

His father looked him over. "Maybe you could bring your boy around this Sunday?"

Joel already had a hand on the doorknob. "I'll have to see about that. I'll talk to you later in the week."

His father watched him from the recliner, gripping the arm rests as if to brace himself for the loneliness that was waiting for him. Joel almost felt sorry as he shut the door.

RETURNS

THIS WAS HOW he left. When Joel was eight years old his father went to work one morning and never came home. It happened on New Year's Eve, three days before his dad's birthday, the year they were hit with a storm that left a quarter inch of ice on the roads and took down tree limbs all across town. His father repaired power lines for Penn Electric, and he was called in to work early that morning because half the county was without electricity. When Joel woke to find hailstones bouncing off the hood of his mom's car it stirred in him the fear that a storm like this could upend their lives for good.

His mother spent the day in the kitchen, listening to an AM station crackling from the radio they kept on top of the refrigerator. Every year they celebrated his father's birthday on New Year's Eve with a big dinner. She put a roast in the oven that afternoon and sat at the kitchen table whispering into her hands, caught up in her own thoughts as if she were hypnotized. It was as if she had known for a long time that something bad was coming down on them and today was the day it was going to hit.

All that week things had been quiet. Christmas was just the four of them. Joel and Derek spent the day playing Nintendo up in Joel's room while his mother holed up in the kitchen and his dad watched television from the living room sofa. A few days later his mother took Derek and Joel to the mall while the holiday sales were still going. They bought his father the leather jacket he'd been wanting, a dress-leather his father called it, something to wear on a night out. His mother seemed to have a hard time deciding. More than once she pulled the same jacket from the rack and held it beneath Joel's chin. It had soft brown leather and a gray satin lining, and before she could put it back Joel tried it on and stood before the mirror, pulling at the sleeves until his hands made it through the cuffs.

"I like this one," he said.

She looked him over. "I'm not sure it's a good idea," she said, which he somehow took to mean any jacket. Then she said, "Okay, off," and brought it to the register.

With the storm raging, Joel went back into the living room to look out the front window. Hailstones jumped off the road like popcorn. Thick cuffs of clear, wet ice coated the power lines and the metal railings along his front steps. He knew his mother was nervous about the storm, afraid his dad might get into an accident or that the weather might make him careless. She had grown up in South Carolina and the thought of battling such harsh weather always made her worry. The previous winter she kept Joel home from school when a quick squall of snow flurries collected at the edge of their lawn, even though it had tapered off long before the bus arrived.

That evening his mother fed them well after dinnertime without setting a plate for herself or his father. She stared out the window as he and Derek ate, though there was nothing to see but a dark, reflective pane of glass. Afterwards Joel took Derek by the hand and brought him upstairs. He put on Nintendo and turned up the volume loud. Derek held the controller, but he wasn't really playing. For each turn he positioned his ship directly in front of an oncoming missile and stared at the explosion of red and orange pixels on the screen. Later, Joel got Derek into his pajamas and laid sleeping bags out on his bedroom floor and he and Derek climbed inside. He could see Derek wide-eyed in the sliver of hallway light, the two of them aware that something in the house was off but unable to figure out what it was.

They listened to the weather tick at the window. After a while their mother came and sat on the bed.

In a voice that didn't seem to come from her, as if it were simply in the air, she said, "Your father isn't coming home."

Derek rose from his sleeping bag and climbed onto her lap.

"What happened?" Joel said, and before she could answer he realized that whatever it was had nothing to do with the storm.

"Nothing happened," his mother said. "He isn't coming back. It's just us now."

"How come?" he said. "How come he won't come home?"

"I don't have an answer for that," she said. "But we're okay. We're fine."

She lay back onto the bed with Derek in her arms and shut her eyes, and then a warmth washed over Joel that made him feel safe from both his parents' problems and the storm outside, as if none of it could touch him as long as the three of them stayed in that room together. He pulled the sleeping bag up over his head and listened to the wind and the rattle of window screens.

WHEN HE WOKE his mother wasn't there. He and Derek went downstairs to find her taking down the Christmas tree lights, tugging at strings of garland and placing ornaments into little boxes. Joel couldn't shake the feeling that everything he loved was coming to a close. He even missed the storm, which had somehow suspended life. Outside his neighbors were cleaning up the mess it had left behind, chopping thick slabs of ice with garden shovels until it separated into pointed shards.

His mother seemed determined to believe what she had said the night before, that they really were fine. He and Derek sat on the couch in their pajamas watching her. When the tree was bare she looked it over with hands on her hips. Then she turned and sat down between them.

"It has nothing to do with you," she said, as if she'd already begun the conversation without them. "Do you understand? Some people have demons and your father is one of them. But it's not about us."

She ran a hand through Derek's hair.

"What are we going to do?" Joel said.

She took his face in her hands. "We keep going. That's the best way. We ride it out until it gets better."

And that's exactly what they did in the weeks that followed: they rode it out. There was school and work and visits to his nana's house in York. Everything kept moving as it did before. Joel went through each day like checking items off a list, hoping the next might bring them closer to seeing his dad again.

On an afternoon bright and cold as chrome, Joel's mother picked him up from school with Derek in the back. She drove to the Langley Mall and parked in the side lot, where there were only a few cars. Then she pulled his father's leather jacket from the trunk. The smell of new leather made him shiver. His dad wasn't coming back, and even if he did his mother wasn't ever going to let things be the same.

Inside she laid the jacket across the counter and asked for a refund. The lady took the receipt without looking at her.

"Is there anything wrong with the garment?" she said.

"No," his mother said.

"Any problems with fit or color or anything. They like us to record a reason."

His mother rifled through her purse as if she needed something right away.

"Credit the damn card," she said. "How's that for a reason?"

And then her purse fell onto the floor and she put a hand over her mouth and cried right there in the store. The saleslady stared for a moment. She came around the counter and put a hand on his mother's shoulder, spoke quietly into her ear. It was the first time Joel had ever seen his mother cry and it frightened him, because with her like this who would look after him and Derek?

IT WAS NEARLY two months to the day when his father showed up at the house. Joel was lying on the floor finishing a math worksheet, waiting for when they would pick Derek up from swim lessons. His father had shaved and his face was chubby and red. He wore dress slacks and cowboy boots and his hair was slicked back as if he'd just come out of the shower. He nodded at his mother as if they'd been talking and had maybe even found some common ground.

When he saw Joel, his father hitched up his pants and said, "Hey there, buddy."

Joel's mother squatted in front of him. "Your father asked if he could come talk to you," she said. "That sound okay?"

It was a question he didn't want to answer. He had spent the past two months keeping an eye out for his father. Some days he raced home from the bus stop and threw open the front door hoping to see him stretched out on the sofa. But he never pictured it like this, his father ringing the bell to his own home, looking clean-shaven and polished like he were trying to impress someone.

"What about Derek?" he said.

"We've got time," she said, then seemed to understand. "Your father will see Derek another day."

She touched the top of his head and left the room.

His father took a seat and asked him to come closer. He started to speak and cut himself off. Then he held up a finger.

"I want to show you something," he said. He parted the blinds so Joel could see a motorcycle parked in the driveway. "It's a Softail. Go on, take a look."

Joel threw on a jacket and went down to the bike. The gas tank was blue with flecks of silver and the fenders had chrome strips down the center. He watched his reflection twist in the exhaust pipes.

"This is yours?" Joel said.

"Belongs to a friend of mine," his father said. "I did some work on the brakes. You can sit on it if you want."

Joel climbed onto the seat and gripped the handlebars. He squeezed the clutch a few times. His father lowered the helmet onto Joel's head and patted it down. "How's it feel?"

"It's heavy," Joel said. "I can't see."

His father grunted. "Yeah, I know. Goddamn helmet laws." He lifted the helmet and wedged it under his arm like a basketball.

"Listen, Joel, I know this can't be easy for you. I've been wanting to come see you for a while." He looked down at his boots as if he wanted to start again. "I can understand if you hate me right now. It wasn't right what I did."

Joel did feel hate sometimes. When Derek fell into one of his whining, pissy little moods, when his mom went off about stuff that didn't matter—getting someplace a few minutes late, a spill on the living room rug—times when he needed his father for balance. But mostly he felt afraid. He was afraid of never seeing his dad again and also that he might try to come back one day, like he was doing right now, and he was afraid of his father, because going away without ever saying goodbye seemed like the worst thing a person could do.

"I'm not making excuses," his father said. "I shouldn't have up and left you boys like that. It's just that sometimes life gets too heavy for you, like you can't carry it around another second." He lifted Joel off the bike. "But that part's over. I won't disappear on you like that again. I wanted to talk to you first. You can understand this stuff better than Derek."

"Are you going to live with us?" Joel said.

His father shook his head. "Me and your mother are way past that. That's not gonna change. Some people don't work together. But that doesn't mean we can't be a family."

In that instant Joel had an overwhelming urge to run. It was like his body needed it the way it needed air.

"Tell you what, I'll pick you boys up on Sunday. We'll do something fun. Whatever you guys want. How's that sound?"

Joel kept his eyes on the ground. He shivered once and his father put an arm around his shoulder.

When his father had gone, Joel and his mother sat facing one another on the sofa, listening to the pendulum clock in the kitchen. Joel had his knees pulled to his chest as he watched her pick at the cuticle on her thumb.

"Do you understand why I agreed to this?" she said. "You boys deserve to have a father. I shouldn't keep him out at your expense. It wouldn't be fair to you."

"What if he leaves again?"

"Let's not think about that," she said. "We'll take this one step at a time."

She pulled him close and Joel leaned stiffly against her.

ON SUNDAY MORNINGS Derek pulled the curtains and stood on the couch waiting for their dad's Monte Carlo to pull in front of the house. He'd been hyper the past few weeks. Twice Joel caught him trying to use his Gameboy, and each time he snatched it back Derek threw a fit until their mother had to separate them.

Derek jumped off the couch and landed so hard it rattled the glass doors of their mother's china cabinet.

"I want to play mini golf today," he said.

"It's raining, Derek."

"Maybe it will stop."

"We're going to the arcade. Dad said I could pick."

The car arrived with the headlights burning dimly through a gray curtain of rain. His mother pulled their jackets from the hall closet and held them in the air. Joel didn't think she was completely sold on these visits. She seemed to be going along for reasons he didn't understand. She opened the door and touched them each on the head.

"You two behave yourselves," she called.

They ran down the front walk ducking beneath the rain. Joel went for the front seat and Derek tried to sneak around him. He grabbed Derek by the hood and pulled him back hard.

"Already with this," his father said, and Derek stomped his feet and got in back.

They drove to a diner in Wethersfield that had a locomotive car attached to the side of the building and a stop light out front that cycled red, yellow, and green. The three of them slid into a large booth where a tiny jukebox was mounted to the wall.

Derek sat next to their father, fidgeting with his jacket zipper until their father said, "If you don't settle down, Derek—" and left it at that.

Joel flipped through songs on the jukebox and Derek reached over him trying to push the buttons.

"Enough," his father said. "You guys are really pushing it this morning."

The waitress stepped up to the table and asked if they needed more time. Her hair was tied back and large silver hoops dangled from her ears.

"Pancakes all around," his father said. "And I'll take a coffee as soon as you can get it here."

"You got it." She looked at Derek and said, "You can go see the train if you want."

"I love a good caboose," his father said, and he shuddered with laughter as she collected the menus and went away.

"Can I go?" Derek said.

"Yeah, go on. Come right back."

When the waitress brought the coffee, his father pulled up his sleeves and tore open packets of sugar three at a time. On his forearm was a tattoo of an old fighter plane Joel had never seen. His father noticed him looking and tugged his sleeve higher.

"That's new," he said.

Beneath the plane were the letters A.M.A., for Academy of Model Aeronautics. His father had always been into RC planes. He built them from kits and had a magazine subscription that still came to the house, but he'd gotten away from it the past few years. There were a couple of partly assembled planes on his workbench in their basement, which was off-limits to him and Derek and they avoided even now.

"Got a couple new planes, too," his father said. He drained half of his coffee and set the cup down hard on the saucer. "Tell you what, why don't we stop by my place after breakfast. You can have a look."

"At your house?"

"My apartment," his father said.

It was strange to hear that his father lived in an apartment. The only apartment he'd known was his Nana's, but that was part of a retirement village.

"You said we could go to the arcade," Joel said.

"We still can. Quit your worrying. You sound like your mother."

The complex was only a few blocks away. His father opened

the apartment door and held it with one arm for the boys to enter first. Inside was a sectional sofa and a television in the corner. Derek ran and jumped face-first onto the cushions.

Joel stood in the doorway because going inside felt like forgiveness. For over two months he tried to imagine where his father was and this was it, an empty one-bedroom apartment only ten minutes from their home. For some reason whenever he thought of his father the backdrop was always a country scene. He imagined acres of farmland, a log cabin with a wood-burning stove. Instead his father was so close Joel was surprised they hadn't run into him getting gas at the Turkey Hill or standing in line at the grocery store. He wondered if his dad had been glancing over his shoulder these past few months, and whether, if they did accidentally meet, he would have stopped or ducked out of sight.

His father went into the closet and came back with a plane resting on his forearms. It had bright yellow wings and a gray fuselage. The propeller had a nick in one of the blades.

Derek reached for the plane and his father lifted it higher in the air.

"Easy with this," he said. "They break. This is just to look at."

He set it on the coffee table and Derek put his face close to peer inside the cockpit.

"Can I see the controls?" Joel said.

"I guess that'd be okay," his father said.

He went back to the closet and pulled a large plastic radio from the top shelf. It was heavy. Joel moved the levers and yanked it away when Derek tried to grab for it.

His father sat on the couch as if he were exhausted. He watched Joel fidget with the radio and rubbed at the stubble on his chin.

"You know, there's another plane in my bedroom," he said. "It's not finished yet, but it's nicer than the one I have here. Why don't you go have a look."

Joel glanced at the bedroom.

"Go on," his father said and put an arm around Derek's waist. "Come here, Derek. I'll show you how this thing works."

Joel opened the bedroom door and found the plane on some milk crates in the corner. It was only partially assembled; the motor lay inside the engine compartment like an exposed heart. He knelt on the floor and turned the prop with his finger, and as he did a rustling sound came from the bed. Hidden beneath a mound of covers was a woman, her long copper hair spilling over the pillow. Joel stood quickly. The woman stretched and made a soft humming noise and was still again.

Back in the living room Derek was leaning against his father's knee. He had the plane by the backbone and was moving it up and down in the air. His father took it out of Derek's hands and set it back on the table.

"Find it?" he said, his eyes still on Derek. Then he patted Derek on the behind. "We can head to the arcade now. I guess we're done here."

A WEEK LATER they went to the shooting range at the Melden Creek Rod and Gun Club. The guy who owned the place had long hair and a triangle of silver whiskers beneath his bottom lip.

When they walked in he threw up his hands and said, "Jack, where the hell you been?"

Right away Joel got the feeling he and Derek weren't welcome.

"These are my boys," his father said.

The man watched them out of the corner of his eye. "They can't shoot," he said.

"I know the rules."

The man wrote something on a piece of paper. Behind him rifles were mounted on the wall like an army ready to advance.

"How long you gonna be?"

"Let's go half an hour. That should do it."

The man put three sets of earmuffs on the counter.

"Enjoy," he said.

They followed their father through the back and down a flight of stairs. He gave them each a set of earmuffs and started going on about the correct way to hold a pistol and how a weapon needed respect and how people who didn't understand that wound up dead from their own stupidity, which was how it should be.

"One less dumb spook, right?" he said. "Good riddance."

Joel didn't want to be there. Earlier that morning he woke with a trembling in his stomach like he sometimes got before school. His legs felt weak. He had gone to his mother and asked if he could stay home and she watched him carefully.

"What's wrong?" she said.

"I just don't feel like it."

She took both of his hands. "I know how hard this is for you. But he's your father and I want you to try. Can you do that for me?"

He wanted to tell her about the woman in his father's bed that morning. It had been in his head all week, but he kept it to himself because he was afraid to hear the words out loud.

His father had them stand against the wall. He flipped a switch and a paper target sailed away from them and flapped in the air when it came to a stop. Derek was wide-eyed.

His father raised the pistol and squeezed off a bunch of rounds. Derek put his hands over the earmuffs and pressed them tight against his head, and when it was over he kept his hands there as if the noise might start again. His father replaced the magazine and set up another target. This time the shots came slower, like he was trying to outdo himself. When it was over he reeled the target back in and yanked it from the clip. He held the two sheets side by side. A few of the shots on the second one were clustered outside the bull's eye.

"Not too bad," he said, and handed one to each of them. "You can keep those."

Joel never understood all the fuss about guns. He had used his friend Evan's BB gun once, lying on their stomachs in the woods behind their school, and it wasn't nearly as fun as he thought it'd be. Evan showed him how to line up the sights and told him to let out all his breath to steady himself before the shot, and they spent the afternoon firing copper BBs into an empty milk container. Each time they finished a full round Evan would run to the target and rattle the tiny pellets in the carton, then he'd count them out to see who was the better shot. None of it excited Joel in the least.

His father signaled him to come closer. He reloaded the magazine and laid the pistol on the shelf with the barrel facing away from them.

"You're up," he said.

"I can't. The guy said."

"It's okay," his father said. "He has to say that."

"I don't want to."

His father's face dropped, and for a moment Joel felt like he'd let him down.

"You don't want to try it? Come on, it's not gonna hurt you."

His father got behind him and lowered his arms over Joel's shoulders. He put the gun in Joel's hands and flipped off the safety.

"You're ready to rock and roll," his father said. "It's going to jerk a bit in your hands, so be ready."

The recoil startled him even though he had prepared for it. But worse was the feeling of the bullet leaving the gun, the lack of control once he touched the trigger. It reminded him of the drop of a rollercoaster, of dreams of falling where he'd jerk himself awake before he hit the ground. He put the pistol on the counter and tried to hide the tears welling in his eyes.

His father laughed from his gut. "It's okay," he said. "You did fine. Hey—"

Joel kept towards the wall, shrugging away from his father's touch.

"Okay, okay. Jesus. You don't need to get so upset all the time."

Joel rubbed his wrist as his father leveled the gun for another go.

AFTERWARDS THEY WENT for pizza at a place called The Shamrock. Joel tried to climb onto one of the stools and his father shooed him off and told him to sit at a table because kids weren't allowed at the bar. He went into the kitchen as if he knew the owner. Through a small window in the door Joel could see him talking to one of the waitresses. She was smiling, glancing back through the glass. The two of them came into the room and she waved and went to the cash register. His father gave her some singles and came back with two handfuls of quarters for the video game in the corner.

"Here," he said. "Make 'em last."

It was an old Donkey Kong machine. The outside was dingy and scuffed and one of the coin slots was covered with masking tape. Joel blocked Derek with his body and put his quarter in first.

"Come on, Joel," Derek said.

"Take turns, guys," his father called. "I don't want to hear any noise."

He grabbed a seat at the bar and the waitress brought him a drink with ice in it.

They burned through the quarters fast because neither of them was any good. Joel came close to saving the lady once, but he was blindsided by a barrel that dropped down the ladder he was climbing. He pounded his fist on the console. He hated these old video games because they weren't fair. Whenever he was about to clear the screen they threw something at him he couldn't avoid. And the closer he got to the lady the more he thought about how difficult it was to pull off, and then if the game didn't turn on him he made some stupid mistake on his own. Game over. But even if he could save the lady that stupid gorilla was going to grab her by the waist and carry her off to the next screen, and then he'd have to do the whole thing over against more impossible odds. The better you did, the harder it got. It was hopeless.

After Derek wasted their last quarter without much effort, Joel asked his father for more. All the guys at the bar fished into their pockets.

"You too, Donny," his father said. "Come on, dig deep."

Donny slid two quarters down the length of the bar.

"Cheap bastard," his father said. Donny flipped him off.

After a few more games the waitress brought out a small pizza and set it on a table close to the machine. Then she brought some napkins and a couple of sodas and pulled out a chair for herself.

"How is it, boys?" she said.

Joel nodded at his plate.

She put a hand beneath his chin and lifted his eyes to hers.

"You look like your father," she said. "I could see it right away."

At the bar his dad had his back to them.

"Do you know who I am?" she said.

Joel shook his head but he'd already pieced it together: the lady in his father's bed that morning.

"My name's Charlotte."

She took a napkin and wiped Derek's face. He squirmed away and ran to their father, who scooped him up onto his lap.

Charlotte watched them a moment, twisted in her chair, then turned back and smiled. She had dark rings beneath her eyes and tiny black gobs of makeup in her lashes.

"I've been wanting to meet you for a long time," she said. "Your dad told me all about you boys. Especially you." She folded her arms. "You having fun today?"

Joel shrugged at the floor.

"Well, your dad is enjoying your visits. I've never seen him so happy. I know—" she said and trailed off. "Look at you. You're a brooder, aren't you? I can tell because I'm the same way. I can think things to death. It's a burden, isn't it? People like us have to go over and over stuff in our head. It never stops."

She slid her chair closer. "Can I tell you something? When I was a little girl I lost my daddy. He was a State Trooper and he was giving someone a ticket on the freeway and was hit by another car. Back then troopers had to wear those big, wide-brimmed hats all the time, and sometimes people would fly by them really close trying to knock it off, you know, with the wind. They did it to be funny. As a joke."

She swiped her hands to show that the car had gotten too close. "Pretty stupid, huh, losing someone like that?"

She shut her eyes a moment, and when she opened them they were heavy and sad.

"What I'm saying is I know what it's like not having a father around. I understand how you felt when your dad was gone, believe me. But you got him back and he isn't going away again. I promise. He loves you boys. He just has trouble when things get difficult. He goes about it the wrong way. Some men are like that. They hold everything inside and when things become hard and they can't hold it in anymore they don't know what to do. They run. It doesn't mean he's bad. He doesn't know any other way. But kids need a father. I told your dad that. I wouldn't stay otherwise. Remember that it has nothing to do with you. Okay?"

His mother had said the same thing—it had nothing to do with him. He thought it was a strange thing to say. His father had chosen some other life over the one he had with them. Even if Joel wasn't the reason his dad left, he still wasn't reason enough to stay.

Someone at the bar called Charlotte's name and she told him to hold on.

"Anyway, I'm glad to finally see you boys." She swallowed hard and came back smiling. "I'd like us to be friends. Do you think that'd be okay?"

Joel watched her shift in the chair.

When he didn't answer she said, "So, what kind of boy are you?"

"What do you mean?"

"Like what are you interested in? You like karate?" She pointed at Joel's T-shirt. It had a decal of two karate guys facing one another, ready to battle. He had no idea where the shirt had come from.

"I'm a ninja," he said.

"A ninja? That's pretty cool."

"I have throwing stars and nunchucks. But mostly I use my hands. I kill people in their sleep. They never even hear me."

He took a huge bite of pizza and chewed with his mouth open. "Oh."

"Sometimes I choke them like this." He put his hands on his throat and made gagging noises as pieces of crust tumbled from his mouth. "There's no blood. No one can catch me that way."

Charlotte opened her mouth but nothing came out. "Joel—"

Joel kicked out his chair hard and dropped another quarter into the game. When the music came up he could see his reflection in the glass. He was smiling in a way the older kids did when they teased someone at school, like they'd done something mean for the fun of it.

"What happened?" he heard his father say.

Charlotte was clearing the plates off the table.

"Nothing," she said. "Everything's fine."

MOVING

ON HIS LAST DAY at Rich's place, Christopher slung a bag
over each shoulder and trekked across town in the afternoon sun. By the time he found his room he was slick with sweat
and had hard knots at the base of his neck. His new roommate,
Shawn, was already settled in when he got there. Christopher
smiled big and shook hands a little too enthusiastically. He never
imagined his roommate might be black. Instead he pictured
someone like his brother, white and suburban and hippy-ish,
and he was mostly jolted by the fact that he had never considered otherwise. Shawn had already unpacked. He had chosen his
bed and his dresser and had his clothes spread out across both
small desks. They stood in the middle of the room and would
have had trouble getting by one another without angling their
bodies.

"Let me show you around," Shawn said. "Over here is the parlor and the formal dining room. Be sure to bring a towel if you
want to use the Jacuzzi."

There were only a few black students at Christopher's high
school and at times he felt guilty for that, as if the lack of diver-
sity in his life made him culpable in the larger problems of race.
The friendships he did have were with a few people he'd met in
class and on sports teams and in church, yet, despite his efforts,
they never seemed to extend beyond the setting in which they'd
begun. The reason was one he had trouble pinning down. Per-

haps it was the frustration of never truly understanding someone who experienced life differently and the feeling that it was easier not to try.

Shawn gestured behind him. "That's my girlfriend, Haley."

Haley lay on the bed, Shawn's bed now, with her back to the wall, turning an old Rubik's Cube between the tips of her index fingers. She had on high-cut jean shorts and her legs were pale and lean. She smiled without showing any teeth.

"You go here, too?" Christopher said.

She nodded. "I'm over in Becker."

"We moved her in this morning," Shawn said. "Her room is bigger than ours. We should file a complaint."

As he threw a pile of clothes onto the bed Haley laid a hand against the back of his thigh and pointed her chin up towards him and they kissed loudly, working their tongues and parting slowly.

Christopher watched them, though he didn't mean to.

When Shawn noticed he said, "Throw my stuff out of the way, man. I didn't know when you'd get in."

"I've been here a few weeks, actually. My brother has a place in town."

"Really. What've you been doing all this time?"

The weeks had gone by faster than Christopher had anticipated. He told Shawn he'd picked up a second-hand copy of *Moby-Dick* at the campus bookstore and had been crawling through it the past few weeks. It was something he had always wanted to read because people said he should. The opening chapters pulled him in right away, but since then he'd been having trouble staying focused, and he knew he probably wouldn't return to it once classes began.

"Does the smell get any easier?" Haley said. She cupped a hand over her nose. "God, it's horrible."

Early on he'd noticed the smell too, especially when the sun heated up the corn fields in early morning, but he'd already gotten used to it.

"It's farm country, babe," Shawn said. "We're surrounded by fertilizer."

"It doesn't smell like fertilizer to me. It smells like vomit. It's sour."

Shawn stroked the back of her neck. "I bet you won't notice after a while."

"You need to build up a callus," Christopher said.

Haley took Shawn's hand. "Can we get something to eat? All I've had was that bagel this morning."

"Let me go for a run first. I haven't worked out in a while."

Haley stood quickly and moved towards the door. "Then come get me," she said.

Shawn latched on to the crook of her arm.

"Can I at least get a kiss?" he said, and the two of them went into the hall.

Christopher could hear them whispering outside. Moments later Shawn came back into the room shaking his head.

"Christ," he said.

"Everything cool?"

"Gonna take some time to get comfortable, that's all. We just drove down from Bridgeport. Corn fields and Amish folks. It's a lot to take in."

"What brought you down here?"

"I got a tuition waiver for the first year. It was a good deal for me."

"Football?" Christopher said.

Shawn laughed a little to himself. "Nah, man, part of the Business program. The Walter E. Leeman Scholarship. One of my teachers told me about it. I organized an after-school program for the younger kids. We did community service, stuff like that."

He grabbed a cell phone off the bed and put it on his dresser. "She always forgets her phone. You got a girlfriend?"

"Had," Christopher said. "She's at Pitt now. We said our good-byes a few weeks ago."

"You miss her?"

"Yeah, sometimes."

But it was more than that. He and Michele had agreed to part ways when Christopher left for Waylan. Neither of them could imagine being a couple so far apart. They worried about temptation and jealousy and resentment, and it seemed the best solution was to separate and see what life away from one another would bring. Christopher was at first excited by the idea. Though he'd never tell her, he wanted to be with other girls, girls who were nothing like her—their personalities, their bodies, their scent. The plan, for him, was to get it out of his system, then return to Michele so they could live the rest of their lives together. If that didn't happen and they wound up moving on, at least they'd avoid slogging through the next few years trying to prove their love was real. It was all very logical and very much planned. Still, she'd been on his mind. He had a nagging desire to show her around Waylan, share every new detail.

Shawn carefully folded an old Iron Maiden T-shirt and placed it in the drawer.

"Me and Haley, we couldn't end it. We figured if it feels right, why not be together? Neither of us wanted to be apart. I think she'll take to this place after a while. That or she'll drag me back home at knifepoint. Either way, problem solved, right?"

At this, Christopher realized, Shawn wasn't laughing.

Later that evening Christopher lay on his bed listening to people pass beneath his window. For the first time since he'd arrived in Waylan he felt alone. The permanence of being here had finally settled on him. He was no longer visiting his brother at school, he was living here, and that simple difference made him desperate for something familiar.

He and Michele had promised not to call one another for the first month. It was Christopher's idea, one that made perfect sense at the time. He was afraid of running to her without ever giving his new life a chance. But he couldn't stop thinking about her body and the sound of her laugh and the way she narrowed her eyes when he teased her. He dialed her number and listened to her voicemail. She'd already changed the outgoing message, which set off a brief sadness inside him. She was doing exactly what they had agreed on, adjusting, moving forward, and he felt cast aside even if he had no right.

Later that night she called him back while he was out for a walk. He was sitting on a hill behind the administration building, looking out over the corn fields. He picked up on the first ring.

"I thought we said no phone calls," she said.

He pictured her lying on her bed, a desk lamp throwing the long shadow of her body against the wall. "I decided to break that rule. It was a stupid rule anyway."

She laughed a little.

"So, how's it going?" he said.

"It's big here."

"Big how? The campus or the city?"

"Both. I feel like I'm in a maze. I'm not used to being around so many people."

"I have the opposite problem," he said.

"You see any Amish yet?"

"Yeah, they're around. And there's lots of corn. I'm looking at some right now. Do you need any?"

"I don't think that's people corn."

"What other kind is there?"

"Feed corn. For animals. It's not the stuff you get in the grocery store."

"I see," he said. "So talk to me. Give me some details."

"No details, really. So far everyone's been nice. I'm actually looking forward to classes. I want to get into a routine."

She wasn't in the mood to talk, he could tell. She was throwing out quick answers like she did when it was late and she wanted to get some sleep. He couldn't blame her. They'd been apart for weeks, had planned for that, and now he was trying to revisit the comfort they'd had in the span of a few minutes.

He was walking now, sweating in the thick humidity. He would go back to his room and crash on his bed and try to put the whole awkward day behind him.

"I wanted to wish you luck," he said.

"Yeah," she said.

"Enjoy your first week."

"You, too. Take care of yourself, Christopher."

"Okay," he said. At the last second he added, "I miss you," but she was already gone.

SUNDAYS

FROM WHERE they were sitting Joel could see the sunfish darting around the bank. It had been a dry summer and the pond was shallower than he remembered. Around it was a ring of mud where the pond had receded, and farther out tall weeds grew up through the water. Across the way some kids were pulling large rocks from the ground and heaving them into the air like a shot put. There were loud, suction-like splashes and the rattle of cicadas.

He and Sam were sitting at one of the picnic tables in the shade, hovering over the checkerboard Joel's mother had given Sam last Christmas. The set had a rodeo theme on the box and plastic horses instead of disks. There were little cowboys to put on the horses' backs when you were kinged. Sam was twisting the leg of one of the men.

"Come on," Joel said. "Pay attention to what you're doing."

Sam put his elbows on the table and leaned directly over the board. His eyes flashed as he moved a piece to open his back row. When he sat back down on the bench Joel's phone lit up and hummed. Lynn. He let it go to voicemail.

"Look," Joel said. He tapped the board. "Hey. Look what's going to happen if you go there."

Sam pulled back the piece. At four he already had a decent understanding of the game, and once in a while he could even see a move or two ahead. But for now he only cared about defense. He liked to move his pieces out of the way when Joel was on the attack.

Then he'd clap his hands and say, "Nope, nope. Not this time, Daddy."

Joel played checkers online all the time and had become pretty good. His buddy Marcus liked to give him shit because it wasn't even chess. He'd tell people Joel was only beating little kids half a world away, eight year olds for all they knew, which may have been true. But Joel loved the simplicity. On a checkerboard all the men were equal. You had to see enough moves ahead and stack your pieces right. Sometimes he liked to begin by giving up one of his men on purpose, just to see if he could battle his way back when the odds were against him. It was about making the right moves when someone was coming after you, not missing anything, and it gave him the same rush he got doing jobs for Dell.

Sam let out a sigh and moved right in Joel's path. His eyes went lazy like he was losing interest.

"Uh oh," Joel said. "Hey. You're walking right into me. Look. Sam, look at this. See what I'm doing?"

Sam was looking towards the pond where the sunnies were nipping at the water's surface, making tiny splashes as they zipped back down. He climbed off the bench and headed towards the water.

"Ho," Joel called. "What's this? We're in the middle of a game, here."

Sam said something about frogs. He knelt down at the edge of the water and peered in. A couple of girls were sitting on the grass nearby. They smiled at Sam the way people did whenever they were out. One of them was barefoot and the bottoms of her feet were the color of ash. The other was wearing a Penn State shirt.

"I think he's done playing," one of them said.

"He gets bored too easy," Joel said. "Takes after his father."

"He's adorable."

"You caught him on a good day," he said.

He wanted to ask if they went to Penn State, anything to keep the conversation going a little longer, but they had already turned back around. His phone went off again and this time he picked up right away.

"Why aren't you answering?" Lynn said. "I hate that."

"We were playing a game. I didn't hear it."

There was rustling on the line as if she moved the phone. "I need you back by five. I'm going to take Sam to my mother's for dinner."

"I told you I would feed him. He wanted McDonald's."

"My mom is leaving for her sister's tomorrow. She won't see him for a few weeks. I don't like him eating that shit, anyway."

"Today is my day."

"Look, I'm not in the mood to argue. Do me this favor, okay? I'll make it up to you next time."

"Okay, okay. We'll head back in a little while."

He'd been trying to keep things peaceful on the hope that she might forget about Florida. His mother was right. She was probably making a point, trying to scare him into being easier to deal with, and if that was what it would take for her to scrap her plans he'd find it in him to be more agreeable. He couldn't risk losing his son. He was afraid of what Sam would become without him, someone too unlike himself, a person he had no hand in shaping. What if Lynn got married down there? The thought of letting some asshole raise him, some suit. How could he hand his boy over to someone like that?

At the edge of the water Sam was still. He slowly raised one of his elbows in the air and turned on his heel. Then he carefully walked towards Joel as if he were balancing a tray of drinks. As he came closer Joel saw a wasp twitching on Sam's sleeve.

"Daddy," he said.

Joel waved his hand and the wasp circled them twice and went away. Sam still had his arm in the air and Joel eased it down for him.

"It's gone," Joel said. "You're okay."

Sam leaned against him. "It was big."

"Mothra big. Swallow you whole."

"I didn't get bit."

Joel held up his palm and Sam slapped it.

"You kept your head. You were stone cold."

"Stone cold," Sam said.

"Like the cool side of the pillow." He tapped the board. "We gonna finish this game or what?"

Sam brought his face close to the board and galloped his horse across the surface. He knocked over a few other pieces and slapped his horse down hard.

"Boo-yah," he said and threw up his arms.

The girls on the grass applauded.

DEMONSTRATIONS

THEY SHOWED UP on a day muggy and overcast, only a couple of weeks into the semester. The man was standing beneath a red maple tree at the north end of the quad, shouting into a bullhorn at the passing students. To Christopher the man looked like a student himself. He wore a hooded sweatshirt and bright running sneakers. He was a day or two unshaven. Yet as Christopher listened, the man seemed to age right in front of him. He spoke with an urgency you didn't find in younger people; he had the cadence of a preacher, but without compassion, without warmth. And there was something off, too. His eyes were set too close, and in his shoulders—low and bony, appearing too frail to carry the weight of his body—he somehow held a frightening potential for energy, like a wound spring, as if a tap on the shoulder might cause some explosive reaction. When Christopher first arrived the man was speaking of sin.

Christopher knew about demonstrations like this. A year ago he'd visited his cousin Aaron at Syracuse, and as the two of them walked across campus they passed an old man speaking to anyone willing to listen. The guy was all collarbone and elbows in a carefully pressed dress shirt. He went on about salvation and the need for Christ in people's lives, how it was never too late to embrace Him.

Aaron said they called him *Bicycle Guy* because of the sky-blue Schwinn he rode to campus each week, how people called out "Hey-Oh, Bicycle Guy" as they passed. He'd become a staple of the university, as much a part of the institution as they were.

"Sure, he's a lunatic," Aaron had said, "but he's our lunatic."

But this man spoke with a ferocity that suggested he was more interested in releasing his anger than offering salvation, and no one seemed to know what to make of it. Even Christopher knew that demonstrations like this didn't happen at Waylan. Some colleges had more of a focus on experience and debate, the exchange of ideas; it was different here. Most of the students he talked to saw college as a means to an end, something you needed to endure to have a better life. Many of them were first generation college students, sons and daughters of blue collar workers who weren't completely sold on the idea of higher education. So why would demonstrators bother with a place like this? Students here were more concerned with modest goals than ideology. The message would be lost. Yet here was this mistreated hound, shouting and carrying on, acting like he'd been horribly wronged and everyone around him was to blame.

Many of the students looked confused. They watched for each other's reactions. Some stared at the ground, embarrassed for the man or afraid to engage. As Christopher moved closer he noticed more people trickling in behind him. The man was pacing as he spoke, much like his professors did at the front of the classroom.

"Drugs and fornication," the man said. "Supporting the murder of unborn souls, homosexuality. Such a life is an affront to God. And not one of you is prepared for your day of judgment." He scanned the crowd to include them all. "Not a single one."

Beside the man, a group of boys were shouting something Christopher couldn't make out. Another guy yelled "smoke a bone" and held a cigarette like a joint. He dragged deeply and blew a plume of smoke in the man's direction.

"And as you continue a life of sin," the man said, "you only move closer to damnation. Now is the time to devote your life to God. Those who do not will be judged."

A woman came from behind him with a sign that said *Choice*

is Death. It had large red lettering and a picture of an aborted fetus.

Christopher turned to find a girl he recognized from his last class. She stood close, as if she were trying to get his attention, and he wondered how long she'd been there.

"What's going on?" she said. She hitched her bag a little higher onto her shoulder.

"Protestors, I guess," Christopher said.

"But why are they here? Protesting what?"

Christopher shook his head.

The wind swept her hair across her eyes and she made no effort to swipe it away. She watched him a moment, as though she were about to say something else, then shouldered her way toward the front of the crowd. Christopher felt he should follow, as if, after their brief conversation, they were now together in this. When they got to the front he felt exposed. The man was only twenty feet away. Christopher didn't know what to do with his hands.

"You're judging us," one student said.

He was tall with silver-rimmed glasses, hair pulled back in a ponytail. His arms were folded and color was bleeding into his face.

For the first time, the man put down the bullhorn. He looked at the student with a steadiness that made Christopher swallow hard.

"What's your name, sir?" the man said.

The student let his arms fall to his sides. "My name's Mike."

The man nodded. "I'm not judging you, Mike. I'm asking you to judge yourself. That's all. I'm asking you to examine your own life. Is that so wrong? The bible says that we should so love God that our love for father and mother and brother and sister should seem like hatred in comparison. Can you say the same?"

"I can say that my beliefs don't involve anyone but myself. I don't judge other people just because I don't agree with them."

"You're judging me right now, sir."

Mike shook his head. "Then we're the same. You're no better than me. Than anyone else here."

"That's true. We're all sinners. Every one of us. I don't claim to be any different. But I've seen what God's love can do, and I've devoted my life to Christ."

"Come on, man. I heard what you've been saying. Jews and Muslims are sinners. Interracial couples. I'm going to hell if I have sex. Do you know how crazy you sound?"

"There's only one path," the man said. "Christ is the only way. You can't obey only the rules you want. That's why I'm here, Mike. That's what you need to understand."

"Just because I don't believe what you believe doesn't mean I'm bad. What gives you the right to shout this stuff at us?"

"It's not about me, Mike. What I think is irrelevant. All that matters are the laws, God's laws. To enter the kingdom of Heaven, one must follow the words of Christ. There is no other way."

"None of that stuff's in the bible," Mike shouted. "You don't know what the fuck you're talking about."

"It's *all* in the bible," the man said. "Every bit of it. Exodus 21, Verse 22, 'If men strive, and hurt a woman with child, so that her fruit depart from her, and yet no mischief follow: he shall be surely punished, according as the woman's husband will lay upon him; and he shall pay as the judges determine.'"

"Yeah, yeah, yeah," Mike said, making his hands into chattering jaws. "You're twisting words around. Around and around with this shit."

"Leviticus 18:2. 'Thou shalt not lie with mankind, as with womankind: it is abomination.'"

"Here we go. Around and around and around."

The crowd had grown so large that Christopher suddenly realized it would be difficult to leave. They were pressed close together and now there was movement, slow, steady pulses, a roiling tide. There was a murmur of voices. Beside him, the girl from class watched the man intently.

"I feel sorry for you," Mike said. He moved closer and was pointing.

The people behind him took up the space; Christopher felt bodies pressed against his back. The crowd cinched around the man and some people called out "Stop!" and "Be cool."

Mike was within arm's length. "You're a hateful piece of shit," he said. "That's all you are."

The man was grinning now, his eyes calm and dismissive. It was a look Christopher had seen before, when someone is trying to trip that switch that makes you lose your composure.

"I've shown you nothing but respect. So which one of us is hateful, Mike, you or me?"

Mike lunged forward and shoved the man into a wall of people. As the guy regained his balance, Mike went for him again, but not before the woman stepped between them using the sign as a shield. He ripped the sign from her hands and stomped it into the ground. Then he reached over her, trying to get at the man, and right then two police officers forced him to the ground. They made him lie on his belly while they cuffed him. Another officer took the man by the elbow and led him away from the crowd, and suddenly it was over. The man was gone; Mike was gone. People stirred, unsure whether to stay or move on. Christopher was still. He watched as the crowd around him slowly loosened its grip, thinning out in spots. Small groups of people huddled together.

The girl from class was still beside him, glassy-eyed. She was breathing heavy.

"Want to get out of here?" she said.

He let her lead the way.

Christopher had no idea where they were headed. As they passed the library they found another demonstrator standing behind a small table. She was small and mousy-looking, with long gray hair knotted in a bun at the back of her head. Before her were two sets of pamphlets: one for Christians, the other sinners.

SHE LED HIM to a coffee shop called Espresso Delight at the corner of Main and College, a small place with a front window so fogged over with steam you couldn't see inside. Christopher pulled an orange juice from the cooler and the girl got a green tea and they grabbed a table in the corner. There was junk tacked all over the walls, hand-written signs on notebook paper, business cards, poorly drawn sketches on napkins; taped to the window sill was a note that said *"Always buy from short guys. They're almost certainly not cops."*

Along the far wall were unframed paintings for sale, each with a note card displaying a title: *After Sunrise, The Last Time I Saw Philly, Dosed.* Student work, Christopher figured. Nothing was over fifty bucks.

They hadn't spoken on the walk over. Christopher stayed in her wake much of the time because she was walking so quickly, but eventually he stopped trying to keep up. She had her head down and it was clear she didn't want to be near anyone right then.

He watched her carefully peel the lid from her cup and blow across the surface. She closed her eyes and inhaled the steam. Then she set the cup down without ever taking a sip. Sticking out of her bag was one of those composition journals with a marbled black and white cover. Christopher wondered if she planned to study, if she wanted him to leave.

She pulled the two pamphlets from her back pocket and flattened out the creases with the palm of her hand. "Which one do you want, sinner or saint?" she said.

"Surprise me," Christopher said.

She slid one to him. "Check it out. It's a test to see if we can get into heaven. The Ten Commandments. Real original."

"It's funny," Christopher said. "Mine only says what *not* to do. Only the bad stuff. There's nothing here about helping people or love or any of that crap."

She craned her neck to read his pamphlet upside down. "Wait, is mine the sinners one? Which one do you have?"

"I think they're pretty much the same," Christopher said.

She took in a long breath and puffed out her cheeks. "Did you see the way the guy was taunting that kid? It was like he *wanted* to get his ass kicked."

Christopher nodded. "I saw it. I think that was part of the plan."

"It's like they're inbred or something. I'm serious. You can tell something's not right by looking at them. Tell me I'm wrong."

She had large, hazel eyes that right then seemed to hold the weight of everything that'd happened. Christopher made the decision not to look into them again. She was working through some kind of episode, one he felt deserved privacy. Behind her was a framed print of solid reds and blues, clean lines with rounded black borders and not a hint of shadow. It had a cartoonish quality, a picture that would fit nicely in a children's book.

"I'm sorry," she said. "It makes me crazy. I don't get people sometimes. It's like I want to shake some sense into them."

Outside some workers were tearing up a small section of road. She watched them carefully, as if she'd never seen such a thing.

"My parents are the same way."

She said this as an explanation, it seemed, for the anger she'd been wrestling with, and he wondered if she had come to Waylan to escape her family only to find other barriers boxing her in.

He stared at the painting behind her and she twisted in her chair to see what he was looking at.

"Owen Turner," she said.

When he didn't respond she said, "The artist? He grew up here. Don't tell me you don't know who he is."

When Christopher shrugged she huffed away her last bit of patience.

"Take a walk with me. I'll show you."

Christopher leaned closer. "You know, I don't even know your name."

She winced a little. "We met in class. That first day."

"I met a lot of people that day. I forgot. I'm sorry."

She folded her arms and there was pity in it. "Well, I'm not going to tell you."

"Come on," he said.

"Sorry. I remember *your* name."

"Is it Dana?" he said.

"Not even close, and don't start guessing. I'm not taking guesses."

She dusted her hands as though she'd been eating something crumby and headed to the restroom without saying so. When she closed the door behind her, Christopher eyed the journal in her bag. All he needed was a name. What was the harm?

On the back cover she'd scrawled "Vampires, Superheroes, and Zombies are Fucking Stupid" in thick black marker. He fanned through the pages. It looked like a creative journal, not so different from the one he used to keep in high school, but the writing was more like a diary, a collection of thoughts. The pages were mostly filled with blurbs, short, reflective sentences, each its own paragraph. The first one was nice: *The hardest I've ever laughed was on a Tuesday.*

WAYLAN LOOKED the way Joel had imagined a college town might look. There were restaurants and convenience stores along the main drag, old fashioned lamp posts and narrow sidewalks. Farther down he spotted a few bars he'd heard about before— Rudy's and The Wayside and The Underground, which had an old neon sign pointing to the concrete steps that led beneath the building. In the span of only a few blocks he passed at least three coffee shops.

It had taken him fifteen minutes to get from the highway to the center of town because nothing was moving. He leaned his head out the window, scanned the line of cars for an accident, hollered "Let's go!" a few times. It didn't appear to be anything but congestion, the gridlock you get leaving a concert. In the car in front of him a girl held a cell phone to her ear. Behind him an old man was hunched over the steering wheel, riding the brake within inches of Joel's bumper. He leaned on the horn and watched them both jump.

They crawled past campus and through an intersection partially blocked with cop cars and finally they started moving again. He drove another half mile like Dell had told him but all he found were homes, an endless string of row houses, tall one-families with sharp peaks and brick facades. After a mile or so he swung the car around and made another pass, and this time he spotted a small entrance at the end of a line of spruce trees. Dell had suggested they meet at the park so Joel wouldn't have to drive all the way out to Hempstead. He mentioned something about waiting by a statue. Joel parked and sat on the hood for a while. Some kids were chasing a black lab around the pee-wee football field, lunging at the dog as it darted beneath their outstretched arms. He'd spent the entire day tearing down drywall and pulling up laminate floors at the job on Hamilton. Now all he wanted was food and a shower and a couple of beers and instead he had to wait on this crazy old man. He hopped off the car and started up the hill with quick, heavy steps.

Some people were playing a doubles match on the tennis courts. Beyond that Joel saw a couple sitting on the grass, about midway up the hill. The girl was hugging her knees.

"Hey," Joel called. "There a statue around here?"

The girl watched him calmly. "I don't know what you mean."

He scanned the field around him. "You sure? I'm supposed to meet someone."

"There's a sculpture," she said, and the kid beside her hitched his thumb back over his shoulder.

Joel spotted a tall skeleton beyond the trees.

"Don't feel bad," the kid said. "I just found out about it myself."

Joel didn't understand what he meant, and he tried to gauge whether the kid was being a wiseass.

Before he could make up his mind, the kid said, "Hey, you wouldn't happen to have a cigarette?" He held up an empty pack and crushed it in his palm.

Joel surprised himself by reaching into his pocket. He shook out a cigarette for the kid and another for himself.

"Many thanks," the kid said.

At the top of the hill, Dell was probably cursing him up and down for being late. Joel decided to make him wait after what it took to get there.

"You guys students?" he said.

The kid nodded slightly, as if he were ashamed to admit it, but the girl didn't respond at all.

"What's with all the traffic?" Joel said. "Is it always like this?"

"No," the kid said. "Cops had to block the roads. There was something going on today."

"What?"

The two glanced at one another.

"We had visitors," the girl said.

It seemed everything they said was an inside joke. Joel stared until the kid began to squirm.

"Some demonstrators were here. Religious types. They got people all fired up."

"What for?" Joel said, and the kid shrugged back at him.

"They were trying to make us like them," the girl said.

He remembered girls like her from high school, the ones he ignored because they didn't have much going on, yet, at the same time, were somehow intimidating, out of his league. He was hovering over her and it seemed she didn't give a damn if he stood there all day.

"So, is this a good school or what?" he said.

He wasn't sure what made a school good or bad. But he knew that, like most things, there were levels, and he wondered where this place fell.

The kid shrugged. "There's better and there's worse. It's not hard to get in or anything."

"You guys get to hang out at the park on a Wednesday afternoon," he said. "Can't be all bad."

"It definitely has its moments," the kid said.

If it came down to it, Joel decided, he could live here. It wasn't a life he would completely take to, but he could do it. By the end of high school he'd become so bored in his classes, so restless, that he had trouble staying in the room. His knee bounced uncontrollably as his teachers droned on. He wanted to get out of school and make money, to stop wasting time. And even after working for the past six years, knowing how it grinds you down a little more each day—your body, your mind, your nerves—he still felt this way. Put him in a classroom and he'd be as miserable as he was back then. But whenever he saw college students he had the urge to prove something, because most of them didn't seem any different from him. Hell, some of them seemed plain stupid, and those were the moments when anger welled inside him. It wasn't that he wanted to go back to school. What he wanted was to show everyone that he could. If he really wanted to he could.

The girl mumbled something and began to gather her things. Joel caught a glimpse of her thighs as she stood, the flesh between them pink from being pressed together. Her legs had a waxy sheen.

"All right, then," Joel said, and started up the hill.

"Thanks for the smoke," the kid called.

The sculpture was made of steel, at least ten feet tall and Ferrari red, and as he moved closer he could see the outline of a person riding the back of an animal, a dog or a wolf, it seemed. Dell was leaning against the concrete base as if to show off his own work of art.

"Nice of you to show up," he said.

"I've been looking for you. You said a statue."

Dell knocked on the dog's foot and it rang like a bell. "What the hell do you call this?"

"That's a sculpture. Not a fucking statue."

Dell cocked his head to the side. "I bet you don't even know who made this."

"Why would I give a damn about that?"

"Because he was a famous artist. Name was Owen Turner. Grew up right around here. He carved this statue."

"It's not a goddamn statue. And since it's metal I'm pretty sure he didn't carve it."

"Christ, it's like a waste of time with you, you know that? There's no getting through."

"Why didn't we meet at your place? You know how long it took me to get here?"

Dell nodded to give him that much. "Yeah, the traffic. But how could I know? I was trying to do you a favor."

"Let's get this over with. I been working all day."

"You know, you don't appreciate nothing. That's your problem. Here." He flipped a key into the air and Joel snatched it before it hit the ground.

"What's this to?"

"A house. It'll get you in the back door."

"Whose house? How'd you get it?"

"Never mind all that," Dell said. "After Saturday, there won't be anyone there for a week. You can go any night."

"You know these people?"

"What's it matter? Do the job I'm paying you to do."

"You're not paying me anything yet. And I like to know who I'm stealing from."

"Look, this is an easy job. I'll give you a grand, clear. You can bring that brother of yours if you want. Grab what I need and go. Don't touch nothing else. Do this right and they won't even notice anything's missing."

"If it's so easy, what do you need me for? Do it yourself."

"I'm too old to be sneaking around like that. That's why I hire guys like you. Here, you'll need this, too."

Dell handed him a scrap of paper with some numbers and an address. The place was in one of the nicer suburbs outside Philly. He'd done some work on a five-bedroom house down there a couple of years ago. Throughout the day he and the other guys had to make runs to the Turkey Hill nearby because the owners wouldn't let them use their bathroom. Joel imagined a big one-family house with a wrap-around porch, one of those cobblestone driveways that arc across the front lawn, the house numbers spelled out in gold script. He stuffed the paper into his pocket, but the address was already in his head. Nineteen-nineteen Berkshire Drive. Kings Row.

RESEARCH

TOM GATTS WAS at the opposite end of the bar, telling Caye, the barmaid, about a guy he knew with something called Cenosillicaphobia, which meant he was afraid—terrified, Tom said—of an empty glass. Caye was half-listening as she counted out the register. But Joel was listening, too, and when he'd had enough he called bullshit.

"It's true," Gatts said. "This guy about loses his mind whenever he sees one. At the bar he frequents, the people know all about it. The bartender makes sure all the glasses have something in them when he's around. It's an honest-to-God condition."

The place was empty enough that Joel could hear the coolers humming below the taps. Gatts was talking so loud the line cook poked his head out from the kitchen to see what was going on.

"Your friend is full of shit," Joel said. "He's trying to get you to buy him a drink."

Gatts was a CNC operator who, years ago, lost a finger running an old milling machine. Joel had heard the story a thousand times, how the long metal shavings snagged onto the rawhide welding glove he was wearing. The threads cinched around his index finger and yanked it off his hand so fast he didn't realize until he saw it spiraling around the bit.

"That finger, it was there one moment and then it wasn't," he said every time he told the story.

"Son," Gatts said, "I'm telling you the God's truth. If it gets to the point where he sees the bottom of a glass he starts to hyperventilate. He said there are times he shits himself it's so bad. He has to use plastic cups at home so he can't see inside."

"What'd I just say? I said bullshit, right? You're either a liar or an idiot for believing it."

"I'm telling you it's the truth, damnit. And I'll tell you what else. You need to watch your tone with me. I don't do things halfway."

Caye held up her hands. "Okay, let's not have this."

"Yeah," Joel said, "come over here so I can shove this bottle halfway up your ass."

Gatts was standing now, wagging his middle finger at Joel while the stump of his index finger wriggled alongside it. "Son, you don't talk to me—"

"Call me son one more time, motherfucker."

"Hey," Caye yelled. "Jesus, Joel, what are you getting so worked up about?"

"How can you stand it?" he said. "Don't you get tired of hearing this shit every day? These guys never know when to shut the hell up. Bad enough I gotta hear it on the job. I gotta hear it here, too?"

She stood before him and placed her hands flat on the bar. "Why don't you call it a night? It's about that time anyway."

"Yeah, go to bed, you little prick," Gatts yelled.

"Tom," Caye said over her shoulder. "Seriously, go home and get some sleep. I got your tab." She shooed him away with her fingers. "Go on. We'll see you tomorrow."

At home he went up to his room and undressed with a mild buzz ringing in his ears. He fired up his computer and played a few games of checkers and all of them were draws. After that he opened a browser and pulled up a search engine. The dumb cracker was right. Cenosillicaphobia was a real thing: *fear of an empty glass; symptoms range from mild discomfort to extreme anxiety.*

But so what if it was true. It didn't change the fact that he spent most of his days around bullshitters and loudmouths, guys who didn't know their ass from a hole in the ground and wanted to talk but not listen. It was enough to make him crazy.

He paused with his fingers hovering above the keys. He had talked to Derek about their next job, made it sound easy, but he knew there was more to it than Dell had made out. He searched *criminal trespassing* and *breaking and entering laws in Pennsylvania* to see what they were looking at if things went bad.

First Degree Burglary in the Commonwealth of Pennsylvania, Chapter 35, Section 3502, a felony. As a first offense, they'd be looking at anywhere from six to forty-five months. Normally he tried not to think of consequences before a job. It could cloud his judgment, make him gun-shy, unable to do what he needed to. But that was before he brought Derek into this. Joel had decided early on that jail was something he could handle if it came to it, but Derek couldn't last in that environment without losing a big piece of himself, and the thought of that sat like a stone in his throat.

Next he did a search for *Owen Turner.* The screen lit up with paintings that looked a lot like the sculpture he'd seen, bright colors and thick black borders and almost no detail. They reminded him of the coloring book pictures Sam made for him sometimes, and he wondered how the guy could get so much credit for doing what was so simple. But he liked the way some of the figures fit together like pieces of a jigsaw puzzle, how the outlines seemed perfect until you looked close enough to see the frayed edges.

There were pictures of Turner himself on the site. He had big eyes and short, veiny arms and coke-bottle glasses with thick rims. There were AIDS ribbons running down the margins, which meant he was queer, probably. A couple of photos had him standing next to Andy Warhol, who Joel knew was from Pittsburgh. But Turner didn't look happy. In every picture he seemed dead inside, like something horrible had gnawed at him for so long he couldn't enjoy any of the success in his life. It was the look of drunks and junkies, a numbness that didn't quite mask the pain you were trying to escape, because no high, not drugs or money or fame, could completely hide the worst shit inside you.

Joel typed *Owen Turner, Waylan*, then backspaced and typed *Waylan University*.

The site came up in sections with rolling pictures of college students on the home page. They were sitting at computer desks and cross-legged on the grass. There was a link for prospective students that took him to program descriptions and pdf. forms and guidelines, and a checklist of things that needed to be done before applying. Joel had never taken the SATs or college prep courses or a foreign language. He didn't even know how to go about getting his high school transcripts. All the hoops they made you jump through just to get in the damn place, and then ten to fifteen grand a year besides, it was all meant to keep people like him out, which was probably how it should be. What business did he have being in a place like that?

He shut down the browser and lay on his bed with the light from the computer screen filling the room. He could hear Derek snoring through the wall. Tomorrow night he'd settle his tab with Caye and leave her a big tip, and if Gatts showed up he'd clap the son of a bitch on the shoulder and buy him a drink, tell him he was only blowing off steam. That was all it was. It happened to everyone.

THE CIRCLE

"YOU NEVER came up that big," Marcus said. "No way."

He gathered the cards from the last hand and speared them into the deck. His cheeks were red and he was talking so much between hands that the game had lost its momentum. It only took a few beers to do him in because he was small. They were sitting at Marcus's kitchen table with Remy and Caroline, who worked with Marcus at the post office.

Joel shifted in the wooden folding chair. "I put some back," he said. "But I was up more than a grand at one point. It was a good table. One guy was wearing sunglasses so I couldn't see his eyes. What a jackass."

The record player was going in the next room, dance music from the 70s, whispery falsettos and big harmonies, guitar sounds like the kind in old pornos. Marcus was into vinyl. He had albums stacked knee-high on his living room floor, all types of music, some of them still in the original cellophane. A couple of the more ridiculous covers hung on the walls in cheap plastic frames: a guy riding the back of an enormous white rat, a hair band looking angrily into the camera, their upper bodies shaved and oiled. Marcus would point them out to his guests and laugh like hell. It was a joke only he got.

Remy flipped off her shoes. She was wearing dark lipstick that smeared the mouth of her beer can. She had pink, pudgy toes, small square teeth.

"It's hot in here," she said, fanning herself with the last hand. "Anyone else hot?"

Marcus opened the back door to let some air into the room.

"I usually play craps," Caroline said.

She had won the last two pots on a couple of nicely-played hands, both times holding back on the flop and the turn and going all-in on the river card.

"I get out to Atlantic City a couple times a year, you know, with my girlfriends, and all they want to do is play the slots. I don't know how anyone can stand those things. There's no game to it. You feed it money and let it decide if you're a winner. You don't even have to pull the lever anymore. Just hit the button. Uh uh, honey, not for me. If I'm going to make a deposit at the casino the least they can do is entertain me. Let me throw the dice once in a while."

"How about tonight?" Marcus said. "This enough entertainment for you?"

He tripped over the word entertainment, adding a few extra syllables.

"You sound like Paul," Caroline said. "Remy, he sounds like Paul."

Remy pointed at Marcus. "Holy shit. Paul. You're Paul."

Marcus froze, the cards a jumbled mess in his hands.

"You've been hanging around that old son of a bitch too long," Caroline said. "You're starting to turn into him."

"Get the hell out of here," Marcus said.

"No, it's true," Remy said. She held up her hands to hold everyone's attention. "'They comin in the night, and they takenin him away.'"

"He doesn't even talk like that," Marcus said. To Joel, he said, "We got this old guy at work. They like rippin' on the way he talks."

"He needs to retire," Caroline said. "The guy's been around way too long."

"He's not that bad," Marcus said.

"He doesn't do a goddamn thing all day," Caroline said. "I

understand loyalty, but sometimes you need to push these old bastards out. People have to clean up his work all the time."

Remy leaned toward Joel, wide-eyed. "'They takenin him away,'" she said.

"And he hides things," Caroline said. "Stupid things. Pens and staplers and rubber stamps. He'll take them right off your work station. What the hell is that about?"

"He's scared they're going to force him out," Marcus said. "How would you feel knowing your days are numbered?"

"Are you kidding?" Caroline said. "I'll be in that place seventeen years this December. Thirteen more and I can retire. You won't see me a day longer."

"When the time comes, it'll be different." Again to Joel, he said, "The guy is from Germany or Austria or some shit. But he doesn't really talk like that. Don't listen to them."

"He does, too," Remy said. "He agrees with you like this: 'Gah huh.'"

Caroline and Marcus repeated the sound on cue.

Marcus dropped the cards in a neat pile. "At break one day he told us this long-ass story about some little kid who was taken away by the Feds."

"'His name Marcus, too,'" Remy said in Paul's accent.

Marcus put a hand over her mouth. She took his arm and kissed the back of his wrist.

"Yeah, that's how the whole conversation got started. So the story goes that this kid, this little Marcus, scribbled something on the blackboard at school, and the teacher saw it and thought it looked like a secret government code. So she called the Feds on him. I know, it's fucking ridiculous, but that's what he said."

Caroline shook her head as if the story saddened her. "How the hell do you call the Feds, anyway?"

"So *then*," Marcus continued, "the Feds came and took the kid and no one ever saw him again."

Remy leaned toward Joel again. "'They cominin in the night and they takenin him away.'"

"That doesn't make any sense," Joel said. "Why would the teacher think it was a code?"

"Dude, don't bother trying to figure it out," Marcus said. "It's all bullshit. The guy likes to tell stories. He wants someone to listen to him."

"Marcus is in love with the old guy because Paul trained him a few years ago," Caroline said. "He's only being sweet."

"I like the guy. So what? I feel bad for him. He's in his seventies, for chrissake. Give him a break."

Caroline put a hand on Joel's arm. "Poor Joel has to listen to us talk shop. I'm sorry. We must be boring the hell out of you. No more talk about work."

She had large round knuckles, long purple nails. Earlier she had caught him checking her out, and since then she'd been making any excuse to touch him, his hands, his arms. At one point she told him to hold still as she combed her fingers through his hair.

"Lint," she'd said.

Marcus stood and stretched his arms up over his head, scraping his chair across the linoleum. The song on the record player had a steady, bouncing rhythm that made even Joel want to tap his foot, and Marcus locked his fingers and began moving his arms in waves. Then he worked a churning motion.

Remy yelled, "Go, baby, go," and Marcus stopped to laugh at himself.

"You coming outside?" he said to Joel.

"Yeah. Get me the hell out of here."

Remy started collecting empties, gently shaking each can to see if there was anything left inside.

"Great," Caroline said. "You gentlemen have a smoke while we clean. You believe this, Remy?"

Outside Marcus lit a cigarette and let it dangle from his mouth as he pissed off the back porch.

"I'm gonna start playing handball," he said over his shoulder. "You should do it with me. It's like twenty bucks a month. That's for everything."

"The hell I want to do that for?" Joel said.

"It's good exercise. I played with this guy from work. You get a good workout."

"I get enough of a workout on the job. The last thing I want to do at night is run around."

"Work is work. It's not exercise. This is good for your head, too. You get out all your aggressions from the day."

"Pass," Joel said.

Marcus watched him as though he were putting together a better argument. He took the cigarette from his mouth.

"I tell you Janine died?"

"Who?"

"My cousin. Remember Janine? She lived over on Pembroke. We used to hang out with her in junior high."

"Shit," Joel said. "Shit."

It was a lifetime ago, when the two of them turned their caps sideways and wore jeans that hung halfway down their asses.

"We used to go to the roller rink."

Marcus tilted back his head. "Jesus, that's right. Every Friday night. My mom would drive us. That's so crazy." He chewed on his bottom lip. "She O.D.'d. They found her on a school playground. She was curled up in one of those big tubes the kids crawl through. Believe that shit?"

"I didn't know she was caught up."

"I hadn't talked to her in a long time. Years. I guess she was hooked up with some scag for a while, but supposedly he's been out the picture. Who the fuck knows. Thing is, they don't know who she was with when she died. Someone had to be with her. And they just left her there."

Joel had come close to kissing Janine once, standing in the cold outside a 7-Eleven. They were waiting on Marcus so the three of them could smoke weed by the creek, and she started telling him about how she planned to move to Montreal one day, a place she'd visited one summer as a kid.

"You wouldn't believe how clean it is there. Every street, every sidewalk. That's where I want to be. Away from this shit."

She motioned to the cars tearing down Hamilton Boulevard and the gray mounds of snow on the curb as if those things didn't exist elsewhere. Then she lit a cigarette and told him how she was going to get a place in the Latin Quarter with her best friend and how the two of them could wait tables or tend bar to get by and that she didn't need anything more than that, only to live in a place that was beautiful. She watched the treetops as she spoke, and when she finished he wanted badly to kiss her. Instead, he stood there with his hands shoved deep into his pockets, the two of them bouncing at the knees and sniffling.

"Where was she living?" Joel said.

"Not sure. The playground wasn't around here, if that's what you're thinking." He leaned against the railing and stared out at the darkness. "They cominin in the night and they takenin him away."

The two of them turned to the sound of the screen door. Caroline stepped onto the porch with a fresh beer in each hand.

"Can I join the gentlemen's club? I want to be with the men."

Marcus held the door for her and stepped back inside. "You be with the man. I'm going inside with the woman."

Joel wanted to follow, but he knew she had come out for him. He had trouble looking at her whenever she spoke. All night she'd been trying too hard to make an impression. She handed him a beer and sidled up close.

"So, what is it with you, honey?" she said.

"What do you mean?"

"Tell me about yourself. Why are you so quiet?"

Joel shrugged. "I'm just hanging out."

"Marcus said you have a little boy."

"Sam. He's four."

"My son's in high school. I remember four. The years go by quick. Your boy's gonna make you old without you realizing it."

"I'm already there," he said. "Trust me."

"You're not with his mother, I take it?"

Joel shook his head. "Not for a while."

"I've been divorced over ten years now. Me and my ex tried to get back together a few times. Seems like every few years we both get lonely enough to try again, long enough for us to get past the hurt we caused one another. After a while it feels like,

What does it matter? You know? But it never lasts. Somehow we always come back to the same issues. Round and round."

He could feel her staring, searching his eyes.

"I was thinking," she said. "Why don't we go for a ride. Give those guys some time alone."

He laughed at first, out of nervousness, maybe embarrassment for the pass she was making. Then she pressed her body against him, leaned a hip against his crotch.

"Come on," she said, and shrugged. "It'll be fun."

He drove to the new housing development across town because he couldn't think of anyplace else. The entire block was being constructed at once, eight houses at a time, for now nothing more than plywood skeletons on muddy, uneven lots. The streetlamps hadn't been raised yet—only the footings were in place—and the neighborhood was dark and private. These homes would sell at around three hundred grand if the market held, but they weren't worth that price. They were nothing more than high-end tract homes, built with the same basic floor plans and cheap forced-air heating systems. Joel felt mild satisfaction knowing there were such big flaws in a home he could never afford.

He swung around the cul-de-sac and killed the engine.

"This the best you can do?" Caroline said.

For the first time all night she seemed nervous, uncertain.

"We framed a few of these houses. No one comes around at night."

Her laughter turned inward, as if she'd stepped back to take a look at herself and was surprised by what she saw. She climbed out of the car, hugging herself against the cool evening, a gesture that made Joel think she would be thin and frail as an old woman. He watched her take small steps around the car, weighing options, Joel figured.

Caroline slid back inside the car and put a hand behind his head and kissed him hard, working her tongue too quickly into his mouth.

She switched on the dome light. "So I can see you," she said, running a hand over his chest.

She started to remove his clothes, slowly, and when Joel tried to help she held his wrists to make him stop. She carefully unfastened the buttons of her blouse, slid from her skirt. She was in good shape—tight round calf muscles, traces of her lowest ribs when she arced her back—though it didn't make her young. She had no curves, none of the softness, the newness of Lynn's body. Her nipples were large and dark and didn't harden beneath the warmth of his hand. The flesh of her belly was loose and dimpled and a thin white scar stretched across the top of her pubic hair. He had a knee on the driver's seat and his shoulders were pressed hard against the roof so that the muscles in his neck burned. He let back his seat as far as it would go and she slid awkwardly over the console and on top of him. She let out a sound from the back of her throat as she guided him inside her.

There was light then, a glint at first, then flashes through the trees. Joel switched off the overhead as a car crawled towards them. It had halogens mounted beneath the grill and Joel could see insects darting through the beams. They hunkered down as the car pulled up alongside them and paused there, whirring with belts. He and Caroline were frozen, breathing into each other's mouths.

"Cops?" she said.

Joel lifted his head. The car had moved to the other side of the cul-de-sac, idling with the headlights off. Then it shut down completely, coughing a moment until it released a final, exhausted shiver.

"Shit," Joel said.

"What's going on?"

"I don't know. Kids, I think."

She shut her eyes. "Perfect. Fucking perfect."

"Hold on," he said.

He was still inside her, but barely, the interruption having drained his body. Caroline lifted her hips and dropped back into the passenger seat.

Outside, all four car doors opened nearly at once. They were definitely high school kids. Boys. Skinny and slouching. They pulled beers from the trunk and carried on as if they hadn't noticed Joel's car at all. He could hear them, though he couldn't make out the words: taunting, rapid-fire voices, high-pitched cackles of laughter.

Caroline felt around for her clothes. "We need to go. Like right now. Fun's over, sweetheart. I'm not putting on a show."

Joel saw one of the boys doubled over with laughter. Another cupped his hands around his mouth.

"Fuck her in the ass," he yelled.

Joel grabbed his jeans off the floor and yanked on one leg, then the other. He pulled on his boots.

Caroline grabbed him by the elbow. "Jesus Christ," she said. "This is embarrassing enough. Let's not make it worse."

He watched himself in the rearview mirror, Caroline beside him, each of them in a place they didn't belong with a person they didn't belong with, getting laughed at by a bunch of kids who probably wouldn't suffer the same fate. He stepped out of the car bare-chested. The boys scattered as he approached, their laughter trailing off as they tried to determine how real this was. Joel hardly looked at their faces.

"We were only messing around," one of them said.

Joel lifted the heel of his boot and brought it down hard against the side-view mirror. It cracked in half and one large piece dangled by a wire.

The kid hollered, "What the fuck? What the fuck?"

He came forward holding up his palms and Joel grabbed him by the jaw and forced him against the hood.

"Come on, man," the kid said. "This is my car."

The other boys had given them space, which surprised Joel. There were four of them. Why didn't they all come at once? The kid in his grasp had a baby face, short hair stiff with gel, both ears pierced. There were some kids you wanted to take the piss out of, who thought they were hard and made you want to smack the taste out of their mouths, but these weren't those kids. He shoved the boy away and headed back to the car.

"Jesus," he heard one of them whisper.

Caroline was dressed when he got back. "Are you crazy?" she said.

"I didn't hurt 'em."

"What the hell were you trying to prove?"

He hadn't meant to scare her. His anger had gotten away from him, and coming out of it was like piecing together events after a night of drinking.

"Bring me back," she said.

"We're going, okay. Calm down."

He put the car in gear and chirped the tires on the way out.

As they sped through the dark streets, he could see her shaking her head, disagreeing with her own thoughts. Then she started to laugh.

"I must be out of my goddamn mind," she whispered.

THE FAIRVIEW apartment building was set with its back to I-67, a neglected four-lane turnpike that jammed much of the day; behind it a tall wooden sound barrier blocked the view of traffic, but from the parking lot you could hear the cars whisking by with rushes of air like gun rapport. Lynn's place was on the third floor, three windows from the end. It was late, but a light was on. Joel could count on that. Lynn rarely slept more than three or four hours a night, and she always kept at least one light burning for when she'd wake. Sometimes, between the dead hours of three and five a.m., she would climb out of bed and carry on as if starting her day. She'd make tea and answer emails, and if she thought she could get in another hour of sleep before daybreak she'd lie back down and give it a try.

The apartment had only one bedroom, which went to Sam. Lynn took the living room sofa, and most nights she drifted in and out of sleep with the television flashing into the morning.

"The TV watches me," she used to tell him.

There were nights late in her pregnancy, during the months they lived in her mother's basement, that Joel would wake to find her clipping coupons in bed, leafing through the circulars she had draped across their bodies.

He put up the car windows and sat for a moment in the quiet. He wasn't sure why he'd come. Everything about him felt unfinished: getting worked up over those kids, quitting mid-way with

Caroline, his last conversation with Lynn. It left him uneasy, and if there was anything he missed about Lynn it was how she could set him right when he needed it.

As he climbed the stairs to Lynn's apartment the echoes of his own footsteps reminded him of his high school corridors. The stairwell smelled of ethnic food, curry and garlic, sharp spices he imagined as oily drops in the air, settling into his jacket so the scent would stay with him for days. Someone's TV sang about "coming down to A-1 Toyota." Earlier, Joel had dropped Caroline off at Marcus's place. She didn't speak as he snaked through the dark roads that led away from the housing development, down past the strip malls and the stop lights on Washington Boulevard, through the narrow, car-lined streets of Marcus's co-op. Caroline kept her hand on the dashboard the entire ride, as if bracing for a sudden stop, though she never put on her seatbelt. Nothing to confine her. When they reached Marcus's place she threw open the door before he had come to a full stop. In his rearview he watched her quicken her pace up the steps.

At Lynn's door he knocked lightly at first, then again with more conviction. He listened for footsteps.

"It's me," he said into the door jam, louder than he'd meant to. He imagined what his voice sounded like from other apartments.

Lynn snapped the locks and yanked open the door. She was in a T-shirt and black yoga pants that showed the curve of her hips, the soft mound between her legs. She hadn't been sleeping, he could tell, but she had been lying down. There were pink blotches on her neck and a thin crease ran down her cheek from a pillowcase seam.

"What the hell?" she said, but her expression quickly softened. "What's wrong?"

"Nothing. Come on, let me in."

"It's late," she said. She looked him over cautiously. "Not if you're fucked up."

"I'm not, okay? I was playing cards with Marcus."

He shouldered his way through the narrow space between her and the door jamb and she shut the door behind him.

She busied herself about the apartment as if he wasn't there, adjusting the pillows, clearing a few plastic cups from the coffee table. Then she disappeared into the kitchen for a while. He moved the blankets off the sofa, all static and body heat. One was a patchwork quilt he recognized from back in high school, the night Lynn showed up at the Shell station where he pumped gas. She had come by a little before closing with half a bottle of Old Grand-Dad and the quilt tucked under her arm. After Joel locked up they climbed over the dumpster in back and onto the roof. Lynn spread out the quilt on the rubbery tar and they lay there tipping back the bottle, staring up at the night sky. Lynn started calling out sounds that turned her on.

"Match strikes," she said. "Body checks in hockey."

"Cracking open a beer," Joel said.

She slapped him on the arm. "Diving into water. The snap of a towel."

"Come closer."

She pushed him away. "Strangers kissing. Walking through snow."

"Okay, okay," he said. "Feedback."

She moved away from him and he caught her gently by the wrist.

"No," he said. "From a microphone. Like right before a concert."

She ran a hand up his leg and began to unbutton the fly of his jeans. "I got chills."

Lynn stepped into the living room twisting her hands in a dish towel.

"You shouldn't be here this late."

She took a seat beside him, though not close.

"I came to see you," he said, half-needling to gauge her reaction.

Since quitting with Caroline he'd been carrying a weight in his groin, the muscles seizing to a tender knot as if he'd pulled something. He ran a hand along Lynn's thigh. The fabric was satiny and tiny fibers snagged the calluses of his palm.

"Don't even think about it," she said, lifting his wrist with two fingers and dropping it onto his lap. She yawned.

Joel adjusted the sofa cushion, which was making a fist against his lower back. "Aren't you going to offer me something?"

"It's late, Joel. Say what you came to say so I can go to sleep."

He reached for her again and she shoved him away hard and slapped his arm for good measure.

"I'm not playing around."

"Jesus, okay," he said.

He watched her dig something from her tear duct.

"Look, if it's about the move we've been through this. Try to understand where I'm coming from."

Joel shook his head. "It doesn't make sense. I need to be able to see my son."

He could see this working on her, the guilt twisting in her mouth, her foot bouncing on the hinge of her ankle.

"I told you," she said. "I'm trying to make our lives better."

"You have other options. You don't need to pack up and leave."

"When opportunities come, you take them, Joel, because they don't come again. My office is going with or without me. There's not much I can do. I can't be without a job."

"Are you fucking your boss? Is that what this is about?"

She let out a breath through her nose. "Brian's like seventy, you asshole."

Then she gave him a shrug that made his balls contract.

"But maybe I am. What's it matter?"

She was never going to budge, not even enough to make him feel like they'd made this decision together. A year from now she'd be down there living a better life than he could imagine.

"Fine. How does Sam feel about all this?"

"What do you mean?"

"Maybe he doesn't want to go. Did you ask him?"

"Kids aren't able to make those decisions. That's a parent's job. That's what you don't get."

"I think we should ask him," he said, and shot up off the couch. "Right now. Let's see what he has to say."

Lynn made no move to stop him. She stared at the floor, working her toes into the carpet.

"Don't," she said softly.

"No, I think he deserves a vote. You're the one always saying we need to talk things out with him. Let's see if he wants to be a thousand miles away from his father. I want to hear it from him."

"I'm warning you," she said.

Sam's room smelled of cheap plastic and laundry detergent. It was stuffy and the walls held a ringing silence as if they were carpeted. He was able to make out his son's shape in the darkness, arms and legs extended, the covers a tangled heap at the foot of the bed.

Joel sat beside him. "Sam," he said loud enough for Lynn to hear in the next room. "Do you want to move far away from Daddy, yes or no? Come on, you have to decide right now."

He shook Sam's shoulder. The boy inhaled deeply, squirming his way out of sleep. He let out a moan and curled into a ball.

Lynn was standing behind him. She had the phone in her hand and she held it up to show him.

"Last chance," she said.

Joel snatched the phone from her and hurled it at the wall. Sam jerked at the noise, and Lynn went to him and began stroking his head.

"It's okay," she whispered.

She glared at Joel. "Jesus, look at yourself."

Joel darted from the room and back through the apartment. He threw open the front door.

"Fucking bullshit," he said.

He slapped his palm hard against the door jamb before stepping into the hallway. The pain went all the way to bone, and then his hand went numb and started to throb. He heard the door shut before he made it to the stairs, the snap of the bolt behind it.

"I'll shut you out," he heard her say. "I will."

FRANCESCA

ON THE WAY to class, Christopher walked past the field house to the crosswalk on Main. A bunch of students waited at the curb as a woman from campus security held the traffic for them. When the first cluster of people stepped into the road, Christopher heard a truck accelerating about half a block away. People at the front stopped at the sound, afraid that the driver didn't see them, and the ones behind them walked into their backs. There was an instant where everyone seemed to consider turning back, but before they could the truck came to an abrupt stop at the edge of the crosswalk. The driver was smiling, and as Christopher stepped back into the road the guy revved his engine like he was about to run them down. Rich had told him some of the locals liked to mess with the students. Old townies, he'd called them. They went to borough council meetings and hollered about the mess students made and the noise and the partying, most of which was true. But what they really hated, Rich said, was the university itself, the fact that it was there at all. It was something they had no use for, and they were afraid it was going to keep growing and growing until one day there'd be nothing left of the town they'd always known.

But Christopher wasn't sure that was the case here. The driver was barrel-chested with a thick beard, eyes puffy and gray. He stared at the crossing guard, a black woman, smiling as if they'd had this exchange before. The woman kept her eyes on him, and when the last students cleared the road the driver tore through the intersection while she was still standing on the yellow divider lines.

The growl of the engine stayed with Christopher as he walked across the quad. He couldn't fight the urge to keep looking over his shoulder as if he were being followed. But by the time he got to the classroom and took a seat he was thinking of Francesca, the girl he'd met at the demonstrations. She had broken down and told him her name at the park, right as they were parting ways.

"It's Francesca, by the way," she said, and she turned and walked up the hill without ever glancing back.

He planned to wave her over to where he was sitting, but she arrived ten minutes into the lesson and took a seat by the door. He watched her throughout class. She was leaning back in her chair with her arms crossed, listening to their professor with a lazy indifference. When class ended, she gathered her things quickly and ducked out before he could make his way through the narrow rows of desks.

Outside he found her sitting on a bench near the library, eyes closed and her face turned toward the sun. She seemed so out of place in Waylan, too worldly for a town like this, too stylish, a person you might find in a black and white magazine advertisement. She was dressed in layers of white, a loose top and a skirt that ended at the knees, small barrettes that pinned the hair off her forehead: a church outfit for a little girl that somehow looked trendy on her. She was pale to the point of appearing delicate and it seemed no amount of sun would change that. He imagined sunburn on her back and her shoulders, the skin a tender pink, peeling away like wet pieces of crepe paper.

"Are you basking?" he said, and she smiled without opening her eyes.

"It's nice to see the sun again. It gets to me after a while."

"Feel like getting something to eat? I'm starving."

"I'm waiting on a friend of mine."

"Okay," Christopher said, and put a hand to his forehead to shade his eyes.

It was early October and the days still held stubborn traces of summer. There was a smell of pollen and cut grass and the dank scent of manure from the corn fields.

Francesca adjusted her skirt to sun more of her legs. "Did you read about the other day?" she said.

Christopher took a seat beside her.

"Those people are suing the school. They go around to different campuses trying to stir things up, and when security makes them leave they sue. It's how they make money."

"How can they sue? Sue for what?"

"The campus is public property. Technically they have a right to be here. But mostly they're after publicity. If they cause enough havoc it makes the local news."

"*That's* why they were here?"

It seemed to Christopher that nothing was genuine. Even in the name of God there were other mechanisms at work, ulterior motives and backroom deals, everyone justifying their own sleights of hand.

"What happened to that guy who was arrested? Mike."

"I'm not sure. I heard two other students were arrested, though. There were problems all over campus. People didn't know how to handle it."

She seemed to have washed her hands of it all, soothed by the fact that the demonstrators were exactly what she thought they were.

At the bottom of the hill a horse and buggy moved slowly along College Boulevard, hugging the curb to leave enough room for cars to pass. Inside an Amish man worked the reins, and beside him a teenage girl held an infant on her lap. Christopher watched the horse clop along the road, head cocked as the cars carefully maneuvered around them.

"I used to dream of horses when I was little," Francesca said. "Talking ones. It's like one moment they'd be horses and the next they'd be people and it would seem perfectly natural."

"You still have them?"

"Not really. But I did have one about a year ago. The horse was talking to me in French. I took four years of it in high school." She started gathering her things. "Here comes Allie," she said.

Allie approached them slowly, as if she wanted Francesca to meet her halfway. Christopher remembered her from orientation, sitting alone and making no effort to meet the other students.

Francesca lifted her bag onto her shoulder. "See you, Christopher."

Christopher remained on the bench. He felt it would look better if he sat there a while. He stretched out both arms.

"Enjoy the sunshine," he said, and he watched the two of them cut across the grass to avoid the shade trees.

HE DECIDED to grab a bite at the diner in town rather than going to the cafeteria. A break was what he needed, from students and campus, from being a part of an institution. Already the routine of college had become tiresome. He needed to get out, eat real food, see ordinary people, if only for a while. These first weeks of his freshman year felt like he was being pulled in all directions at once. His professors made passionate arguments to major in their area of study. When he walked across campus students shouted recruitment slogans to join clubs and political organizations. With so much opportunity before him, he felt as rudderless as he did in high school. How could he be expected to find a single thread-like path out of a tangle of endless possibilities? Some nights he dreamed it was the last day of the semester and he had yet to show up to class. Other times his dreams put him inside a dark, nebulous vacuum that felt like he was suspended in space. The more he tried to move, the more he remained in place, rotating slowly in a directionless void. What he wanted more than anything during these dreams was to be contained, to feel the pull of gravity and the weight of a lead blanket over his body, to be secured. He'd wake in a dizzying panic with his arms outstretched, reaching desperately for something to grasp.

The diner was a small building with dinged aluminum siding and a curved ceiling that gave it the look of a subway car. On weekend mornings people stood single-file on the sidewalk waiting to get in. He sat at the counter, ordered an omelet and watched the cook pour an enormous bowl of eggs onto the grill. When they were done, the waitress dropped the heaping plate of food before him, sending a few of the potatoes tumbling onto the counter.

Outside, the same horse and buggy he and Francesca had seen earlier was parked at the curb. His mother had such love for the Amish. Their house was decorated with hand-made quilts and hex signs and a wooden rocking horse she'd bought at a farmhouse years ago. When he was twelve, his parents took him to Lancaster for a long weekend. They toured an Amish home (not a real one, but a replica for the tourists) where a high school girl with a tiny diamond stud in her nose told them about the Amish lifestyle. He wondered if he could live in such a world, if he would bolt at Rumspringa, and if he did, where he would go. What options were there for a kid with an eighth grade education and no money, not even loved ones to help him get started? He decided he would never be able to survive such odds, and it left him with flashes of pity whenever he saw the Amish going about their lives.

Christopher finished about a quarter of the food, paid his check and headed outside, glad to be away from the smell of the griddle. The Amish man was stacking empty wooden crates back into his cart, hobbling as he worked. One of his legs was several inches shorter than the other and his shoe had a thick rubber sole to compensate. When the man noticed him watching, they both turned away.

He walked through the fairgrounds and alongside the creek, which had swelled from the past few weeks of rain. The water spun in small eddies at the edge of the footbridge. For days he'd been fighting the urge to call Michele. Whenever he thought of her he felt a shadow of envy, the sense that she was living a better, more exciting life while he had hardly moved at all. He liked it here, but he didn't expect to feel so hollow and alone without her. For the first time he understood her need for wanting more.

After a while the sound of rushing water made him have to pee, and he cut down one of the alleys towards Rich's place. He found his brother in the backyard, swinging at the ground with a large pickaxe.

"What's going on?" Christopher said.

Rich looked up as if his brother had been there the whole time. He leaned the pickaxe against his hip.

"Pig roast, my brother! Pig roast! Week from Saturday. I was going to give you a call. We're going to cook the motherfucker right in the ground."

"Where the hell did you get a pig?"

"We didn't yet. Friend of a friend of mine works for a butcher." He wiped his forehead. "What brings you here?"

"Killing time before class. I was in the neighborhood, as they say."

Rich held out the axe. "In that case, think you can spell me for a bit?"

Christopher was happy to take a few swings. It felt good to give his body some work. The ground was much harder than he expected, filled with large stones. When he was able to break through, the axe pulled up narrow strips of earth that immediately collapsed in on themselves.

"Don't you have a shovel?"

"No. Maybe I can borrow one," Rich said. His eyes had a rheumy glaze, and he stared at the hole as if something were about to happen.

Christopher dropped the axe. "This isn't working. Maybe your neighbor has some tools?"

"I need to get to work, anyway. What the hell time is it?"

"All right. I'm gonna use your bathroom, then. I'm dying over here."

Rich made a sweeping "be my guest" sort of motion with his arm.

"Saturday after next," he said. "Bring whoever you want."

The house was quiet, which made Christopher feel a little more alone. He stepped into the bathroom and shut the door, splashed some cold water on his face. Then he leaned towards the mirror and wondered about choices. Outside, the pickaxe rang like a game of horseshoes.

WORK

AT THE HAMILTON SITE, they tore down a wall that separated the kitchen and dining room and patched up long, rectangular gaps of sheetrock like missing teeth. Bobby Gillespie, their supervisor, had pulled Derek from another job to help. They were going with new molding throughout the house because the old stuff was cheap, and all of it needed to be finished by the end of the week so the subcontractors could lay new hardwood. It was their usual routine. Tear it down, haul it out, patch it up. That was Joel's livelihood. He'd gotten to a point where he didn't have to think.

He set Derek up with Charlie, who was a good worker, unlike a lot of the guys Joel worked with. One guy named Marcel used to go outside every time his cell phone rang, and Joel would find him pacing in the shade, head down as if the conversation were important. Another guy used to eat his lunch in the passenger seat of his car and would come back smelling of booze. Most of them didn't last. The three of them were moving pretty good until Derek came up short on two of the cuts, and Charlie stepped in to help because Joel was too annoyed to deal with it.

The house reeked. On the first day they pulled up the carpets to find narrow gray trails of dried cat piss all over the subfloors. Even with the carpets gone and the windows open Joel could taste ammonia at the back of his throat.

At lunch, Charlie grabbed a few empty compound buckets and set them upside down in the living room so they could sit. All day he'd been calling them The Brothers Martin.

"I get to work with The Brothers Martin today," he kept saying. "That's all right."

Charlie held a wad of tinfoil out to Joel. "Give this a try. It's cold, but it's good."

"What is it?"

"Chicken and rice and some other stuff. Here."

"Nah, I'm okay," Joel said.

"Try it, man. I made it myself."

"You cook, Charlie?" Derek said.

"Yeah, I cook. Why are you surprised?"

"Who taught you?" Derek said.

"Nobody taught me. Take some, for Christ's sake."

"Why are you always trying to give me food?" Joel said. "I have my own lunch."

"Because you need to try new things, open your mind a little. Right, Derek?"

"My mind's okay," Joel said. "Get that shit away from me. It smells worse than this house."

"Derek?" Charlie said.

"I'm good."

Charlie wagged his head. "The Brothers Martin," he said.

Derek had beads of sweat running down the length of his jaw. He was constantly overheating. It was like a coil burned in the center of his body, glowing orange like those old dashboard cigarette lighters, making his face and his ears red, dotting his upper lip with moisture.

"You talk to Marcus about next week?" he said.

"I forgot," Joel said. "I'll call him."

"What's next week?" Charlie said.

"Going out," Derek said through a mouthful of food. "My birthday."

"How old you gonna be?"

"Twenty-two," Derek said.

"Shit, I got shoes older than that. Where you going?"

"I don't know," Derek said. "We'll probably hit the bars."

"What you want to hang out with Joel for? Why don't you take out some nice young lady?"

"You should come with us," Derek said. "You can buy me drinks."

"I'm in bed by nine o'clock, man. Besides, I don't go to your places."

Joel was amazed at how easily Derek and Charlie got along, how they spoke like friends. The closest he and Charlie ever came to that was when they were working and got into a zone, one steadying a piece of sheetrock while the other put in the first screws, moving with precision, warning each other when they'd backed up too far or if the seam had dropped. They were co-workers, not friends, which seemed right to Joel.

After they finished eating, Derek and Charlie went back to work and Joel stepped outside for a cigarette. A warm breeze picked up and Joel had to hunch forward and cup his hands around the lighter so it would catch. When he lifted his eyes, Bobby was pulling in front of the house. He rifled through some papers on the passenger seat and poked at his phone for a while. Then he stepped from the car and came up the walk with a clipboard in his hand. He was dressed like a high school gym teacher: polo shirt tucked into a pair of track pants, white running sneakers with reflective strips of silver and blue.

"How's it going?" he said.

Joel sucked deeply at the cigarette and nodded.

"Goin' all right," he croaked through an exhalation of smoke.

He opened the door for Bobby and followed him inside.

Bobby started scanning the place right away. He ran a hand along the door molding and checked the corner seams with his thumb. He felt the drywall with his palm.

"Where are we today?"

Joel showed him around. They were further behind than even he had realized.

"Will you guys be finished by the end of the day?" Bobby said.

"Not the way we're going," Joel said.

Bobby shook his head. "You'll need to come in tomorrow, then."

"Goddamnit."

Bobby held up his hands. "Look at the situation you're putting me in. I got guys coming. It's not like we can tell them to wait."

"I can't tomorrow," Joel said.

Bobby looked up from his clipboard. "Government jobs are your problem, not mine. This comes first."

He meant side jobs. That's what they called them, though Joel never understood why. But Joel had never mentioned side work before.

"I got my kid tomorrow," Joel said. This was a lie.

Bobby shrugged. "Sounds like that's your motivation, then. Asses and elbows."

Bobby checked a few more of the trim joints, which weren't as clean as they could have been. He dusted off his hands.

"Look, I don't like coming down on you, but that's the situation. We're staying on schedule, so it's up to you how this gets done. Either step it up today or come in tomorrow to finish. Those are your choices."

Joel held his tongue. If they came in tomorrow it would only be for a few hours and no one would be looking over his shoulder. And he could always use the overtime. At least there was that.

IN THE MORNING Joel and Derek got to the house a little after eight. Charlie was parked out front as they pulled in, listening to his car radio with the windows down. He held up his watch to say he'd been waiting. Joel flipped him off.

They had double-timed it the previous afternoon and all that was left was the trim in the two bedrooms. The morning was moving fast; they'd be out by noon, eleven-thirty if the three of them kept their heads down. Derek and Joel took measurements and made cuts and leaned the crown molding against the walls for Charlie to nail in place. Charlie measured out the baseboard and the quarter round to be set after the floors were finished.

Joel had trouble with one corner because the room wasn't exactly square, which happened with some of these older houses. It took him three cuts to get it right, and as he checked the seams Derek came up behind him.

"Some guy's at the door. Says he needs to talk to you."

"Who is it?"

"Didn't say."

Joel found the guy standing on the front steps, waiting like it was Joel's house and he needed permission to come inside. He wore a button-down shirt tucked neatly into his blue jeans, which had been ironed with a crease running down the front legs. He handed Joel a large manila envelope.

"Joel Martin?" he said.

"Yeah, who are you?"

"My name's Carl Singer. I'm from the Westborough County Sheriff's office. You've just been served a temporary restraining order."

Joel checked to see if anyone was behind him. "Why am I getting a restraining order?"

"All the information is there. The instructions are inside. You'll need to appear before the judge in a few weeks. The court date is listed."

"Come on, what's this about? I haven't done anything wrong."

"Do you understand the information I've given you?"

"No, I don't understand. I don't understand any of this."

"You'll have an opportunity to tell your side to the judge. For now, you need to cease all contact with this person."

"This is crazy. She's out to make me fucking miserable. You don't know her."

The guy nodded like they were suddenly on the same side.

"Look, son, you don't want to make this worse. The best advice I can give you is to get it taken care of. Just follow the instructions. Getting angry will only give you more hoops to jump through. You need to do what's right."

Joel folded the envelope into a thick wad and stuffed it into his back pocket.

"She's taking my son away from me. That sound right to you?"

The guy nodded again. "No. No it doesn't. But I've been doing this long enough to know something brought me to you, and you'll need to take responsibility for that. Eventually we all have to answer for the choices we make. Understand what I'm saying to you?"

Joel took a breath. "Yeah, all right."

"Good luck to you, son. I hope things work out."

ARLENE WAS at the window when they pulled up. She wished today had been one of her work-Saturdays. She was barely through her coffee when the sheriff arrived earlier that morning asking for Joel, politely, as if out of genuine concern. She knew what it meant, but she went along anyway, telling him how to contact Joel's employer and track him down. They would have found him eventually. Better to get it done quickly. But she was nervous about talking to Joel and she needed to talk. She was certain she could help if only he'd let her.

She had picked up fresh cold cuts for the boys, honey-baked ham and provolone cheese, thinly sliced turkey and deli pickles. She used to do this on Saturdays when they were young. Back then both her boys were late sleepers. They'd wake after eleven with puffy eyes and matted hair and go right for the kitchen table. It was something she missed, watching them happy for the weekend and fighting over the last slices of cheese.

As soon as he saw her, Joel held up a hand. "I don't want to hear it," he said. "Don't even start with me."

"Let's sit down," Arlene said. "I have food. Why don't you both come and eat."

Derek went straight for the kitchen as Joel eyed her carefully. "I don't want you up my ass the whole time," he said, and followed.

At the table the two of them dove in. Joel piled thick cuts of meat onto a roll and lowered a slice into his mouth. He mashed the sandwich flat until huge gobs of mayo curled out the sides.

"I should've never went there," he offered. "It was late and I was pissed off about Florida and I should have stayed clear. But she didn't have to go and do this."

"What did you expect?" Derek said. "She works for a god-damn lawyer. It probably took her all of five minutes."

"Maybe she's making a point," Arlene said. "She could still stop this."

"You should talk to her," Derek said. "Apologize. Tell her it won't happen again. You don't want this going to court."

"I can't," Joel said. "That's the whole point. I can't go near her. She can have me arrested."

"I'm not saying go there. Call her up. I bet you could straighten it out if you talk to her."

"I can't have any contact. None. What part of that don't you understand?"

"Both of you, stop it," Arlene said. "Joel, I can talk to her if you like. If you want me to stay out of it I will, but I think it might do some good. Lynn and I always got on okay. It's up to you. I won't mention it again."

She listened to the sound of Derek chewing. Joel nodded at his plate.

"Okay," he said.

And the way his voice fell she almost thought she heard a hint of gratitude.

GOVERNMENT JOBS

THE SUN WAS a dull copper, softened enough by the horizon that he could watch it duck behind the treetops. Joel had worked in neighborhoods like this before, wide, quiet streets with not one car parked on the road, enormous front lawns mowed in careful rows, bushes trimmed in odd, twisted shapes, the whole street well-kept but appearing almost abandoned. There were no sidewalks, no traffic, no kids playing in the yards. It was as if the street were a movie set, the homes nothing more than thin sheets of plywood propped up with two-by-fours.

"That's the one," Joel said. "Right there."

The house was a brick colonial with black shutters and a red front door, simple compared to some of the other homes in the area. He could see a small gazebo off the patio in back, the kind you see in wedding photos. Behind it was a long stretch of woods, and beyond that was an elementary school he'd spotted on the drive in. Perfect, so far. Dell had made the job sound easy and he was starting to believe it.

"We can park at the school and come in through the back," Joel said.

"You sure you can turn off the alarm?"

"He gave me the code, Derek. Worry about what you need to do."

"So what now?"

"We'll need to wait a while. The later the better."

He drove up and down side streets and then made his way through the business district. Derek put his head back and nodded off for a while as they cruised past the high school and the shopping mall, and when he woke he asked Joel to stop so they could eat. They found a sports bar called Bleachers in a strip mall on the other end of town. Inside there were TVs on each wall and two behind the bar. They grabbed one of the high tables in the corner, ordered a couple of drafts. Derek asked for some wings, but Joel knew he'd have to fight to get them down. He didn't like having so much downtime before a job. It was easy to overthink, to second-guess his instincts. The stress trembled in his bowels.

He felt good when they first looked at the place, but the longer Joel sat there, the more impossible the job seemed. Dell had them going after an old pocket watch, an antique, worth thousands, he'd said. How were they going to find something that small scrambling around in the dark? They could spend hours searching the house in broad daylight and still come up empty. But Dell swore they'd find it in an old jewelry cabinet in the upstairs bedroom. He was sure of it.

The waitress came back with their food and Joel waited for her to leave.

"We'll hit the upstairs first," he said. "Then we can work our way down towards the exit if we need to. I don't want to be in there more than a few minutes."

Derek was hunched over the basket of wings, sucking orange grease from his fingertips. He was calmer than Joel expected.

"I can't watch over you the whole time," Joel said.

"I know that."

"I'm saying you'll need to think for yourself. Both of us need to. If anything happens you get the hell out. Don't worry about me. Understand? You get your ass back to the car."

"I won't stay a second longer than I have to. Trust me."

"I do trust you. You hear me? I'm trusting you with this."

Derek slumped back in his chair. "I hear you," he said.

Joel threw back the rest of his beer and signaled the waitress for another round. On the television behind the bar was a commercial for a new show on the Science Channel. A few weeks ago they aired a five-part series on the universe and Joel had watched every episode. They talked about quarks and nebulas, discussed time as if it were a wire you could bend into any shape you wanted. He thought that because it was a television show everything would make sense by the end, the way stories did. Instead he was left confused and frustrated, unable to piece together any useful information. He didn't think he was stupid. He was merely missing the basics, stuff he should have learned years ago, and sometimes it made him feel like there was a curtain between himself and the complexities of the world and that no matter how long he lived he would never really understand what was on the other side.

By eleven-thirty they were the only ones left in the place. The Packers game was over and their waitress had already left for the night.

The bartender stood before them and clapped her hands together. "Anything else I can get you guys?" she said.

"No," Joel said. "I guess it's about that time."

He paid the bill and she unlocked the front door to let them out. When they got to the car, he turned to watch the lights inside shutting down one section at a time. They were ready, probably more ready than any job Joel had ever done, yet he still felt like he was pulling something heavy behind him. He tried to shake the negativity from his head. Think too much about missing your target and you will. Every time. He imagined the staircase and the jewelry cabinet and the pocket watch lying inside the open drawer, and he repeated these thoughts as he drove through town listening to the sound of his tires against the road and the click of his turn signal.

At the elementary school, Joel cut the lights and pulled around to the back lot. They sat in the car a moment, silently gearing up while the engine ticked itself cool. Joel opened the glove compartment and pulled out a couple of pen lights he'd bought at a gas station. At home he'd put a couple of layers of scotch tape over the bulbs to dull the light even more.

He handed one to Derek. "Only when you need it," he said. "Light travels forever."

Derek gave it three quick flashes. "I'll try not to use it at all."

"You feeling okay?" Joel said.

Derek already had one leg out of the car. "Let's just do it."

They tramped through the woods single file, Derek following in Joel's footsteps, his hand resting lightly on Joel's back. Joel could see only a foot or two ahead of him but it was enough to maneuver through the growth. As kids they loved to play in the woods like this, dressed in camouflage and army boots, taking cover behind trees with toy pistols. He still liked the smell of decay in the woods, dead leaves and grass, mud. Breathing it in now made him feel safe.

They made their way to a path that Joel hoped would lead straight towards the house, but that was a guess. There was a chance they'd come up short. After a few minutes of pushing forward, Joel felt they should have met the clearing. He wondered if what he thought was a straight path was actually a lazy arc that was, by now, leading them in the opposite direction. He stopped to get his bearings and Derek waved him forward to say they were okay. Joel felt a strange sense of pride from this. They were communicating without words, reading each other's movements.

They found the clearing moments later. Not far away was a house with a few lights on upstairs. Joel heard movement out by the patio, and beneath the porch light he saw a dog raise its head, one of those small, mangy little things. They froze, then backed away from the clearing so they could move farther up the block, but not before the dog came charging, the sound of the chain's slack being taken up, the dog's bark giving way to a yelp once the tether caught. They kept the same steady pace until the barking stopped. Joel caught the peak of the gazebo farther down, and he pointed so Derek would know where they were headed.

At the edge of the clearing, the two of them stood and listened. There was a light wind and the rustle of leaves. Joel counted backwards from ten. With a nod they snuck across the lawn.

When they reached the back door Joel fished into his pocket

for the key. The dog was a few houses down, a good fifty yards away, but it still had a bead on them. It began to bark again, more frantic now, pulling at the chain and taking halted leaps forward. The key slid easily into the lock, but it wouldn't turn. He worked it in each direction as the dog kept on, scrambling around the patio. Suddenly, with the whoosh of a sliding door, a woman stepped outside and clapped her hands twice. He and Derek froze beneath the blanket of darkness.

"Louie," she yelled, and for a moment the dog stopped.

Then it started again, still aimed at them, and the woman looked in their direction too. She took the dog by the collar and guided it towards the house.

"Inside," she said and pulled the door behind her.

Derek moved him aside. He pulled hard on the door handle and worked the key until the latch released. The two of them slipped inside and shut the door.

There was a faint squeal, like the flat-line of an EKG, though not the alarm itself. Joel went right for the glowing blue keypad beside the light switch and punched in the code Dell had given him. He tasted bile in his throat and hit the numbers in again, faster this time. Then he pushed the clear button on the bottom corner and tried once more. The noise ended with a final chirp. They were standing beside two front-load washers, exactly as Dell had said.

Inside they caught a break. There were nightlights plugged into the hallway wall sockets, flat, neon-blue disks that created almost no shadows, giving off enough light to get through the house without bumping into things. Derek headed upstairs with Joel close behind. They started in the master bedroom, which smelled faintly of perfume. Joel pulled the drawers two at a time and ran his hands across the bottom while Derek searched the walk-in closet. There was no jewelry cabinet that Joel could see. He tried the nightstands and the dressers again, and when he finished he moved to the next room.

There were only a few pieces of furniture here, a bed and two large dressers—a spare bedroom, he figured. He searched the first dresser on his knees, pulling drawers from top to bottom until the entire unit tilted forward from the weight. He braced the dresser with his shoulder and set it back on its base.

The other two bedrooms were kids' rooms. He took a quick look and went back to find Derek.

"Anything?" he called, bolder now, speaking barely above a whisper.

"Not yet," he heard from the closet. "Gimme one more minute."

"One more," Joel said. "I'm going down."

Joel went down the stairs and into an office beside the living room. He sat in the soft leather chair and pulled the desk drawers. He was making more noise now, maybe panicking a little, and he forced himself to stop and take a breath. On top of the desk was a framed picture, and he held it beneath the window to catch some of the streetlight. It was a family portrait, the parents and two boys, all of them flashing the same empty smile. They looked like churchgoers, happy and respectable, proper, but beneath that was a strained look of constipation, as if they were struggling to hide all the twisted and horrible parts of themselves, the parts that made them human.

The woman had an expression that reminded him of his mother, the way she seemed to paralyze every muscle in pictures. Joel couldn't tell if she was happy or if her life was coming apart or if she was somewhere in between. And there was something else about her, something familiar. Her eyes, the sharp corners of her mouth. Joel felt his heart stammer. He slammed the picture onto the desk and darted from the room.

"Derek," he called up the stairs. "Let's get the fuck out of here."

Outside there was a quick flash of headlights, the whispering shriek of old brake pads. He ran to the window to find a squad car parked at the crest of the driveway, one solid red and blue light burning on the roof.

In a surge that made his legs feel watery, Joel hissed, "Derek, cops."

He rushed to the back door and paused a moment and called Derek again, and when there was no response Joel pulled open the door and went out.

He darted across the lawn at full speed and slipped back into the cover of the woods. At the edge of the lawn he crouched down into the brush. The officer was still sitting in the idling squad car, reading something under the dome light. Joel watched the upstairs windows.

"Come on," he whispered.

He reached for his cell phone and hit Derek's number. It rang and rang and rang.

DEREK'S STOMACH ROLLED. The windows glowed from the headlights outside. He knew what it meant, but instead of running he sat on the corner of the bed and listened for voices. His arms and legs prickled like they'd been asleep and were slowly coming back to life. He would sit and wait for the rest to come to him. He'd heard the cop try the front door moments ago, switching the handle back and forth, following procedure. For now the call was a false alarm, but he'd get inside eventually, and then Derek would call out, gently, so the rest could happen without a struggle.

But it was all moving too slow. He heard voices outside, the officer's and a lady's, probably the one with the dog, and when he couldn't take the waiting another second he got to his feet and made his way down the stairs. He walked through the entryway and into a small room by the kitchen. Joel was out, probably sprinting through the woods on his way to the car by now, cursing him for lagging behind, for trusting him when they both knew Derek couldn't come through in a situation like this.

The far window looked out to the side lot where two fat bushes blocked much of the view. The room would get almost no sunlight during the day, and while coming away from that thought, Derek lifted the sash and climbed over the sill. He lowered himself onto the ground and suddenly he was outside, standing beneath the cover of the enormous shrubs, amazed he had slipped out so easily. He could hear the cop on the opposite side of the house. From here the woods were only thirty feet away, and without hesitating he snuck across the lawn.

He could see them now. The lady was wearing pajama bottoms and a windbreaker and her hair was tied up at the top of her head. She was trying different keys in the door he and Joel had gone through only a short while ago, and when they went inside Derek bolted for the car.

He stumbled twice, the second time rolling his ankle and nearly going chin-first onto the earth. He pushed through a thick patch of thorns—heart pounding, his ankle throbbing—until he emerged on the far side of the parking lot. He turned once and put his hands on his knees, then straightened and turned again. The car was gone. Joel. He left.

JOEL POUNDED the steering wheel with the heel of his palm. His jeans were damp to the knees and hitchhiker thorns clung to his socks and the laces of his sneakers. He turned onto the entrance ramp and got on the dark, narrow stretch of turnpike. He needed to get the car away from there, to widen the distance between himself and Derek and the law. There was nothing else he could do. They probably had him by now. They'd take him in and process him and put him in a cell with drunks and dealers to take the piss out of him, but there wouldn't be much fight in Derek. It wouldn't be long before the police pressed him enough to retrace his steps back to Joel. And then Lynn would use this in court as one more example of how she was right about him. He was a fuckup, an unfit father. Now he was a criminal, too.

Joel realized he'd only turned on his dashboard lights, and when he switched on the headlamps it was like waking from the syrupy fog of anesthesia. He tried Derek's cell again. Like before, the phone rang until it switched over to voicemail. All he could see were the fan of his headlights on the road, beyond that nothing but a wall of darkness that seemed to cinch around him. Suddenly his phone lit up on the passenger seat.

"Joel," Derek said. He was breathing hard into the phone.

"Where the fuck are you?"

There was rustling and the sound of air. "Jesus, Joel. Don't leave me here. Please don't leave."

DAYLIGHT

SHAWN AND HALEY were fucking a few feet away. They liked to have sex, slow and quiet, in the first moments of daylight, a time they probably figured Christopher would be in his deepest sleep.

Christopher could hear their mouths going at it, the soft coos as Haley tried to stifle her breathing. She'd been staying over at least three or four nights a week, the two of them spooning in that tiny bed. He watched them through the shadow of his own lashes, imagining Haley naked and warm beneath the covers. He wondered if their bodies fit the way he did with Michele. Listening to them always brought him back to her, her soft belly against his, the way she tipped back her head when he was inside her. Sometimes he tried to imagine Francesca, but it wasn't the same. She was hazy and transparent, ghostly, which made it feel too unreal. He had to rely on imagination rather than memory and it created too much distance to get him excited, like when he dreamed of being with a movie star.

They finished with a shudder. Christopher could hear Haley whispering something into Shawn's ear as he lay dead-weighted on top of her. They untangled their bodies and were still, and after a while Christopher was able to clear his mind and slip back into sleep.

When he woke Shawn wasn't there. Haley was sitting on top of the covers, dressed and hunched over Shawn's laptop. She looked in his direction when he swung his feet to the floor.

"Shawn went to the gym," she said.

"Okay."

He was tired of seeing her around, and for spite he imagined her having sex only a few hours before. He threw on some jeans and a fresh T-shirt and rummaged through his bottom drawer for clean socks. As he was pulling them on he realized she was still watching him.

"Did Shawn ever talk to you?" she said.

"What do you mean?"

"Those people who were here. Did he say anything?"

Somehow he knew what she meant, the demonstrators who were on campus a few weeks ago.

"Not to me."

"You heard about it, right?"

"I was there. It was pretty crazy."

She closed the laptop. "Shawn got into it with one of them. We were holding hands and some asshole started talking shit. He called us interracial breeders. I mean, what the fuck?"

Christopher thought about the guy he'd seen revving his engine at the crosswalk a while back, but he didn't want to believe that kind of hate existed in this town.

"Those people were railing against pretty much everything. It's hard to take them seriously."

"Shawn should'a laid him out. I would have loved to see that."

She was looking directly into his eyes and her focus made him uneasy. Then she turned away.

"That smell is sludge, you know. That's what they call it. It's cheap fertilizer made from waste. Pretty much anything that goes down your drain. They say it's safe, but they've had trouble with the water out here. I've been trying not to drink from the tap."

Christopher stopped tying his laces. "I've never heard of that."

"It's true," she said. She watched him again. "I hate it here, Christopher. It's like this place is backwards."

"I wouldn't worry about those people. They're not even from here. I heard they go from one campus to the next."

"It's not that," she said.

But he understood. There was a mild hostility in this town that he had trouble putting his finger on, and lately he'd decided it had to do with fear, the fear that things were changing for the worse and that the students were somehow to blame.

He could see that whatever small connection they'd made was over. She opened the laptop and waited for the screen to come up.

"Will you be here when Shawn gets back?" he said. "I don't want to leave the door unlocked."

"I can go."

She put on a pair of flip-flops and jammed some clothes into a small canvas bag. Then she folded the shirt she had worn to bed, rich with the scent of her body, he imagined, and left it on Shawn's pillow.

HE HAD FOUND Derek at a gas station a few blocks from the elementary school. As he pulled up Derek stepped out from behind a dumpster and got in. His hood was up and his face was red to the eyes. Inside the car he smelled of earth and body heat. Neither of them said anything until they reached the highway. Then Derek let out a long breath and Joel asked if he was okay.

"Where the fuck were you?" Derek said.

"You weren't answering your phone. I kept calling."

"You said to get back to the car. That's what I did."

"We've been through this. Things go wrong. I had no way of knowing what was going on."

"You coulda' gave me a chance."

"How long was I supposed to wait, Derek? Ten minutes? Half an hour?"

Derek lowered the window and turned his face to the wind. The fresh air made Joel's body feel heavy. They'd pulled through a bad situation; and even though it was for nothing, he had an exhausted feeling of accomplishment, the high of wriggling from the law's grip. His heart slowed for the first time all night. Twice he caught himself dozing as he stared at the flashing white lane markers, and when they got home he went straight to his room and collapsed face-down on the bed.

HE WOKE TO the sound of Blue Oyster Cult blaring from his alarm clock. His eyes were tacky and stinging, his stomach achingly empty. He could hear cabinet doors and the clatter of dishes downstairs, the water rattling pipes in the walls. With his head still in a fog, he had an intense need to see Derek. He'd slept like the dead since they got back, and coming out of it made him paranoid, as if something happened while he was out. He threw on some clothes and flew down the stairs. Derek was sitting at the kitchen table, hunched over a bowl of cereal.

Joel pulled out a chair and sat.

"Everything's cool," he said, though he wasn't sure why.

He watched Derek shovel cereal into his mouth with loud slurping noises.

"So, you gonna tell me how you got out of there?"

"The window," Derek said.

Joel waited for more but there wasn't any.

"You're saying you walked right by them?"

"Pretty much."

He realized he was laughing, a trembling kind of laugh like when you stub a toe.

"The cop never saw you?"

"I'm here, ain't I?"

"Jesus. You must be the luckiest son of a bitch ever."

Derek lifted his eyes. He got up from the table favoring one leg.

"Look, I'm sorry, okay? I didn't know what to do. I was calling you the whole time."

"Yeah, you told me."

"What's wrong with your leg?"

"What do you think?" Derek said.

He decided to leave it alone. Derek had come within inches of having a criminal record and jail time. It had to be a hell of a tweak.

"I guess we're okay, then," Joel said.

"Yeah."

"We got away with one."

"We're great."

WITH THE HAMILTON JOB turned over to subcontractors, Joel had to meet Bobby Gillespie at a house in Levins. When he pulled up Bobby was standing in the driveway talking on his cell phone. Joel stepped out of the car and into the morning chill.

Bobby clapped his phone shut. "You look like holy hell."

"Rough night's sleep."

"Well, get it together. I need you to demo the bathroom by the end of the day."

"Am I alone?"

"For now. You can hold off on the tub. Haul what you can out to the driveway. I'll have Charlie come down later with a truck. He can help you with the heavy stuff."

They did a walkthrough while Bobby tapped a pen against his clipboard. The place was a shithole and was going to stay that way. The kitchen was clean but outdated, with pressboard cabinets and Formica countertops and an ugly green and white linoleum floor. The owners were having the upstairs bathroom redone with cheap ceramic tiles and fixtures that wouldn't last ten years, all to make it look presentable for a quick sell. In and out.

"We're on a five-day schedule, so let's have it done in four."

"It'll be tight," Joel said.

"You can handle it. I'll be back tomorrow to see how things are going." He looked Joel over. "You know, you really do look like shit. I don't care what else you got going on so long as you come here ready to work. You're no good to me like this."

"What the hell are you talking about?"

"I'm saying I need you sharp."

He followed Bobby back through the house and outside. At the curb Bobby opened his car door and stood in the space between.

"Hey, let me ask you something," he said. "You and your wife have been separated a while now, right?"

"She's not my wife."

"But you guys are split?"

Joel nodded.

"She ever put ideas in your boy's head?" Bobby said.

"Like what?"

"Stuff about you. She ever make you out to be the villain?"

It was something he wondered about, whether Lynn had it in her to fill Sam's head with that kind of poison. He thought about breaking points.

"I don't want to talk about that," he said.

Bobby nodded for a while. "It's my little girl. She looks at me different now. Like she knows about the worst parts of me, things a kid shouldn't have to worry about. You ever get that?"

Joel shook his head.

"Maybe I'm getting paranoid," he said. He knocked on the roof of his car and climbed inside. "Don't fall asleep on me."

Joel watched him pull away. When the car was out of sight he went back inside and hunkered down in a corner of the upstairs hallway. He shut his eyes and disappeared.

AFTER WORK Joel made the trek out to Dell's place. He found the old man at the back of the house, power-washing an enormous blue tarp that was stretched across the ground. He had already made three narrow gashes from holding the wand too close. Joel picked up a rock and skimmed it across the tarp and Dell turned and shut down the compressor.

The motor sputtered to a stop and all that was left was the sound of a hard wind pushing through the trees.

"It was your daughter's house, wasn't it? You had me stealing from your own family."

Dell took off his cap and scratched the top of his head. He used his shirt sleeve to dab at his tear ducts.

"Some day you're going to learn to stay out of my business."

"The neighbors saw us. We were almost arrested."

Dell worked his jaw a moment. "I take it that means you didn't bring me my watch."

"There was no watch. There was nothing in there."

Dell smacked his cap across his knee and mumbled something at the sky.

"Didn't you check the bedroom?"

"Every drawer. You gave us bad information."

Dell shook his head. "You must have missed it."

"We looked everywhere. We were blindsided."

"Well, hell, there's no guarantees. You should of dealt with it. These jobs never go perfect."

"I can't find something that's not there. Shit, we could be in jail right now. Over a stupid fucking watch."

"That watch is nearly a hundred years old. It was made in Switzerland, for chrissakes. My daddy bought that watch when he was stationed overseas."

"So what."

"So I should be the one to have it, not Ellie. Who do you think took care of him all those years? He left it to her so he could have one last laugh at me. Now she'll never give it up."

"You were looking to sell that thing as soon as you got your hands on it. Don't act like it means more than that."

Dell leveled his eyes with a soberness Joel had never seen in him.

"Let's get one thing straight, son. You're a crook like me. You can pretend otherwise, but it's true. There ain't no difference between us."

"Maybe you're right about that," Joel said. "But I did the job and now you're gonna pay me."

"How can I pay you? Pay you for what?"

"You sent us into a bad situation. You had us looking for something that wasn't there. I don't take that kind of risk for nothing."

"I can't pay you without the merchandise. Where's the money gonna come from?"

Joel stepped forward. "Look, you can give me my money or I can take it out of your ass."

"That right?" Dell glanced at the house and Joel stepped into his line of sight.

"Forget your gun, old man. It ain't gonna happen."

Dell put down the wand. "Tell you what, here's what *is* gonna happen. You're gonna get off my property and we're gonna forget this whole conversation ever happened. Because you think you know everything, but really you don't know shit. All it takes is a phone call to throw a wrench into your whole life. That brother of yours, too."

Electricity prickled across Joel's scalp.

"How the hell do you think I found you, anyway? Those guys you work with had you pegged for a thief from the minute they saw you. It was them who brought you in, not me."

"Who? Who brought me in?"

Dell swatted at the air. "What difference does that make? You didn't exactly go kicking and screaming. Look, this is how it is. I mean, what kind of business did you think you were involved in?"

Joel backed away. He got into his car and tore out of there kicking up gravel and a cloud of dust. Dell was smarter than he'd given him credit. He was thinking ten moves ahead and had been since the beginning. Joel's own bosses—Bobby and fuck knew who else—had pulled him into a business that was bigger and grimier than he'd realized, and they'd gone with him because they figured he was smart enough to pull off these jobs but not enough to realize they were using him. Derek was right: it was more than stealing. They were taking from anyone they could, working guys, family. No one was off limits, and now they were turning on him, too. The whole world was crooked, every son of a bitch that walked the earth.

RUNNING

THE DEW DAMPENED the toes of Christopher's sneakers as they jogged across the grass. They ran past the old water tower and got on a trail that sliced through the woods, then hooked back towards the football field and hit the track for a while. About mid-way into the third lap Christopher put his hands on his knees and breathed fire. Shawn slowed to a walk when he noticed. He came back around and slapped Christopher on the back.

"You're out of gas already?"

"Getting my legs back. Give me a second."

"Legs my ass. Those cigarettes are messing you up."

Shawn leaned forward and gagged a little. He arced his back and spit out a thin stream of pink bile.

"Fuck. I'm draggin' myself. Too much Jäger. Shit is evil."

Christopher heard him come in the night before, struggling with the lock and fumbling around the room with the lights off. The music bleeding from his ear buds sounded like sleigh bells from across the room. Shawn crashed down hard on his bed, whispering lyrics until he fell asleep.

"You were in a bad way last night," Christopher said.

"Off my ass." He lay back on the bleachers and pulled at the crook of his knee. "Me and Haley went to that keg crawl. I thought it would be good to get out and meet some people. It was a madhouse, man. Then we had it out, me and her. It was a bad night."

"What happened?"

"She was hanging at my side the whole time, you know? Like she didn't want to be there. And then I was talking to some girl from class and that was it." He sat up. "She's been miserable. It's driving me crazy."

"She told me you almost beat the piss out of one of those demonstrators a few weeks ago."

"She said that?"

"She was afraid they got to you."

Shawn shook his head. "Not me. *Her.* She was screaming in the guy's face. I practically had to carry her away." He thought a moment. "The thing is, I don't know what the big deal was. A few yahoos come onto campus and everyone loses their shit. Did you see those people? Who gives a fuck what they think? Bunch of racist bullshit. One guy was trying to tell me heavy metal was a sin. Are you fucking kidding me?"

"It was hard to ignore. I can understand getting rattled by it."

"I guess that's true. You know, we get looks from people, me and her. You believe that?"

"It's the townies," Christopher said. "We all get that."

Shawn dropped his shoulders and sucked at his back teeth.

Christopher nodded. "I get what you're saying."

"I mean, last week at Sheetz the cashier put my change on the counter instead of in my hand. It's not a big deal, but what the hell." He shook his head to chase those thoughts from his mind. "It's got Haley all wound up. I don't know. Maybe you had it right breaking it off with your girl. I feel like I'm constantly trying to hold things together."

"I've been wondering if that was the right move. I can't get Michele out of my head."

"So go see her already. Shit, I'll lend you my car for the sake of some lovin'."

Christopher had considered taking the bus for a long weekend, but he worried about what he'd find—her independence, her happiness, a life without him.

"We promised to give each other some space."

Shawn brought his head down to his knees and stretched the muscles in his neck. "You're a stronger man than I." He put a hand on the back of his head and gripped his chin with the other and turned until there was a sharp pop.

"You guys should come to my brother's place," Christopher said. "Maybe Haley needs a different crowd."

"We'll probably lay low tonight. There's some bad things going on in my bowels right now. You bringing that girl?"

"Francesca. Yeah, she's coming."

"Francesca," he said, drawing out her name. "What's she like?"

"It's a good question. She's not like anything."

"Those are the ones that get you," Shawn said. He stood and started bouncing on the balls of his feet. "You better watch yourself, man. She'll be deep under your skin in no time. Mark my words. After tonight you're done for."

DISGUISE

JOEL TOOK the ride home from work with the radio blaring. He was in exactly the mood to cut up, to tune out all the noise in his head and laugh for a change. He and Charlie were able to drag out the week and pull an easy work Saturday, doing the final odds and ends at the Levins job: changing the electrical outlets, grouting the shower tiles. They could have been done days ago, but Bobby hadn't been riding them like usual. He came by early Thursday morning with a couple of egg sandwiches for the two of them. Joel worried about what it meant. If Dell had talked to him he was trying not to show it, which could itself be a warning, a way to keep Joel guessing.

When he got home he could hear the upstairs shower going. Derek had been avoiding him all week, but he'd come around after a few drinks. Joel grabbed a beer from the refrigerator and drained half the can leaning against the counter. Through the window he could see his mother in the back yard. She was sitting in a lawn chair at the edge of the patio, in a coat too heavy for the time of year. She didn't turn as he came out the back door.

"You two going out?" she said.

"That's the plan."

Daylight Savings was in a couple of weeks and the sun was small and pale, as if it were running out of fuel. His mother was doing that thing with her hands, rubbing each fingertip against her thumb then starting again. He felt sorry for her sometimes. He and Derek were pretty much all she had, two boys who would all but drop out of her life once they had the means. Then what would she be left with? She'd spent her entire life focused on getting by, surviving for another day, never taking a risk or trying for something more, and this was where it got her.

"I called Lynn today," she said.

"And?"

"Wasn't good. She was barely willing to speak to me. Did you really do that stuff, Joel? Throwing things? Punching the walls?"

"She's making this worse than it was."

His mother frowned as if he'd said something hateful. "She won't put up with it anymore. You shouldn't have been there like that. You've got to use your head. She's not putting up with it anymore."

"How many times you gonna say that?"

"I'm worried, Joel. There's something different about her this time. You'll need to find yourself a lawyer. She's not going to back down on this one. Otherwise you're going to lose that boy for good."

Joel spat at the lawn. "I can't afford a lawyer."

"She's scared, Joel. I'd be scared too if I were her. I would."

"Whose side are you on?"

"There's no sides. This isn't some game. You need to start getting your life in order."

"Most of my money goes to her. I do my part."

"It's not enough. That boy deserves more." She shook her head. "You'd better start thinking twice from now on. You've used up all your chances."

"All I want is to see my kid."

"Then you need to be smart. Your way isn't working."

Upstairs he filled the sink with hot water and wiped the steam from the bathroom mirror. He evened out his sideburns with the electric trimmer and lathered up to shave. With half his face done he leaned against the vanity. He could see traces of his father, the veined gray rings beneath his eyes, a tuft of wiry chest hair peeking over his collar, gravity pulling at his cheeks, his old man's scowl. In a few years he'd be like those angry old fucks on the job, fat and leather-skinned, bitching like he was the only one living the right way, sticking to the same sad routine. He was losing his son and it didn't seem anything would change that. He'd fight with everything he had, but there wasn't much in the way of hope. Lynn had made him out to be a monster. *Look at yourself,* she'd said that night, holding onto Sam as if Joel were about to do him harm. His own son.

"Yeah, look at me," he said, and he brought the trimmers up before he had the chance to change his mind.

DEREK NEVER cracked a smile. He only glanced at Joel long enough to say "Je-sus" as he got in the car. He'd been giving Joel one word answers all week.

"You gonna mope around all night?" Joel said.

Derek shrugged at the road. "Why the fuck not? It's my birthday."

Derek messed with the radio the whole ride and finally settled on a classic rock station you could barely make out through the static. They pulled in front of Marcus's place and Joel hit the horn. Marcus made it as far as the bottom step before doubling over with laughter.

"What the hell did you do?"

Joel felt the top of his head out of self-consciousness. Earlier, as he watched himself in the mirror, he felt like a cartoon character. He had shaved the sides of his head nearly down to the scalp, leaving the center long like those shampoo Mohawks he and Derek gave themselves in the tub as kids. He considered bringing up the clippers to finish the job, mowing the center band so he'd be left with a buzz cut, but after staring at himself for a while he found someone he didn't recognize and he liked the way that felt.

"You look like a fucking rooster," Marcus said.

"Just get in the car."

Marcus slipped into the back seat and put Derek in a sleeper hold. "Happy Birthday, asshole."

"Get the hell off me," Derek said.

"There's dollar drafts at Helwig's," Marcus said. He was leaning forward between the seats. "We should head there first."

"We're not going to Helwig's," Joel said.

"Where are we going?" Derek said.

"Don't worry about it. I got it covered." He clapped Derek on the shoulder. "I figured we'd try something different for a change."

Marcus pulled out a one-hitter and started loading it up. He passed it to Derek, who dragged on it pretty good and tapped the ash out the window.

"Caroline's been asking about you," Marcus said, holding the smoke in his lungs. He released with a burst of laughter and coughed hard.

"Suck on it," Joel said.

Marcus hit Derek on the arm. "Hey, your brother's got a thing for MILFs. Did you know that?" He reloaded the bat and sent it forward.

Joel had gotten off easy so far. Marcus had been ripping on him for hooking up with Caroline, but only that. It made him wonder how much of the story Caroline left out to save herself the embarrassment, even if that meant letting Joel save face too.

Marcus and Derek got quiet as they barreled down the highway. Their heads bobbed to the radio. They drove past the hospital and the weigh station where the state troopers liked to snag people on radar, and then the horizon stretched out before them, rolling hills and wide plots of farmland that went on for miles. Joel took the exit for Route 211, which led straight into Waylan.

"Where the hell are we?" Derek said.

"We're in the country," Joel said.

"Why did we come all the way out here?"

"College chicks," Joel said. "A change of pace."

"I don't see any college," Derek said.

"Or chicks," Marcus said.

"Trust me."

They drove through town with the windows down and a crisp breeze circling the car. Joel had been thinking about this night all week. He usually avoided college girls. Sometimes he'd throw them hard looks, like when he saw people in suits going to work in the morning. It was a way to show he wasn't like them and didn't want to be, to look down at them before they had the chance to do the same. But talking to those kids at the park made him feel a little less out of place, and he'd been thinking how some of these girls might even like him because he was different from the guys they already knew. He pulled into the back lot and found a space by the door.

"Doesn't look like much is going on," Marcus said.

"It's early," Joel said.

Inside, The Underground wasn't much different than the bars they usually hit—cement floor, a low bar against the wall, couple of pool tables in back. The three of them ordered beers and shots of Smirnoff that came in little plastic cups. Marcus shouted happy birthday at the ceiling and the three of them tipped back the shots. They listened to Daltrey sing about love raining down. Joel ordered another round and Marcus got off his stool and starting swaying with the music a little, not at all in time. He walked to a table in the corner where a couple of girls were drinking bright pink cocktails. Joel could see him introducing himself and the girls responding.

Joel got quarters from the bartender and motioned towards the pool tables in back. "Come on," he said over his shoulder.

He racked and told Derek to break, and Derek came at the balls from the side and scratched. Joel put the cue back on the table and racked them again, tighter this time, and Derek aimed dead center and dropped a couple of low balls. Neither of them was any good. They had a cheap plywood-top table in their basement (it was still down there, dusty and warped, boxes of Christmas decorations stacked on the surface), and every once in a while when they were kids the two of them would start practicing in the hope of getting better. It never lasted. Eventually they would get frustrated with the delicate geometry, at having to worry about not only sinking the shot but also setting up the cue for the next one, and soon he and Derek would be arguing, shoving the balls across the table to see if they could make them collide with enough force to send them flying through the air.

"You ever go see Dell?" Derek said.

Joel was surprised to hear him bring it up. "Yeah. The son of a bitch wouldn't budge."

"Nothing? After all that?"

Joel bounced the rubber end of his cue off the floor.

"Shit. You should have caved his head in."

"I thought about it. He's more connected than I realized."

"Well I'm out. This shit ain't worth it."

Joel wasn't about to argue, not now. Hell, he felt the same way, though he wasn't sure it would hold.

The first game took forever. They both had trouble shooting straight, but finally Derek sunk the eight and Joel told him nice game and grabbed a couple more beers. The next game went much faster. Joel was running the table pretty good until he scratched on a shot he should have tried to bank. A few turns later he scratched on the eight, and he dropped his stick on the table to show he was done for the night.

Marcus was still at it. When they got to him he was firing questions at the girls, listening closely as they answered, watching their eyes. He was good at talking to girls because he never seemed to want anything more than conversation, and maybe he didn't. Girls didn't get uncomfortable with Marcus the way they did with Joel, that nervous laugh to fill the silences, their bodies turned enough to let him know they wanted to be somewhere else.

"Ladies, this is Joel," Marcus said. "He's in a punk band. They'll be performing later tonight."

The girls lifted their eyes to the top of Joel's head, then turned back to Marcus with an awkward smile.

"This here's Teresa and Beth. They're in the master's program here. They're nurses."

"Physician Assistants," Teresa said.

"Right," Marcus said. "My mistake." He put an arm around Derek. "And this here's Derek. Today's his birthday."

Teresa tilted her head. "Is it really your birthday? I can't tell when he's serious."

Derek nodded. "It's true."

"I don't believe you," she said. "Show me your license."

Derek reached for his wallet and handed it over. She held it under the recessed light that hung directly above them. Rainbow-colored flecks of hologram flashed from beneath the laminate.

"You look like a little boy in this picture," she said.

She handed his license to the other girl.

Derek's body jerked as he tried to muffle a huge belch. "I was supposed to get it renewed already. Good thing they didn't card me."

Marcus slapped his license on the table. "Okay, everybody throw 'em down. Let's see whose is most embarrassing."

Joel played along, and when Beth picked up his license she said, "My God, our birthdays are a day apart. What hospital were you born in?"

"Langley," he said.

She grabbed onto Teresa's wrist as if this were too much for her. "Me too. That means we were in the nursery at the same time." She looked around the table. "Am I the only one who finds that unbelievable?"

"It's pretty amazing," Joel said, and meant it, not because they'd been born at the same time and place, but that now, all these years later, they'd run into each other and realized it.

The odds seemed impossible, like life had already been mapped out and he was merely walking a path that had been set for him, held in by guardrails that made sure he couldn't veer off in another direction. It was reassuring in a way. All he had to do was keep moving forward.

MARCUS TRIED to talk the girls into sticking around but they were bent on leaving. About that time the place started to fill. Joel hung back in the corner for a while, watching the room as if he wasn't a part of it. In the opposite corner people were throwing darts, guys against girls. Some jock with keys dangling from a cord around his neck made his way through the crowd and two girls hopped off their bar stools with a shriek and hugged him. Marcus and Derek had lapped him on beers and were almost ready for another, and Joel could feel the three of them receding further into the background.

Marcus slipped away to take a piss. Derek was in a conversation with some guy about the Phillies, which Joel had never heard him talk about before. Joel hated sports. When the Eagles games were on at the Windsock he secretly rooted against them. It wasn't because he disliked the team; he didn't give a damn either way. What he hated were the people rooting for them, those sad, fat sons of bitches high-fiving like grade school kids, their girlfriends who wore Eagles jerseys and sweat pants and screeched at every play, all of them wasting their time with something that didn't matter. It was pathetic, and he loved to watch their disappointment when their team lost.

When the guy left, Derek leaned against the wall cross-armed, watching the room like a security guard waiting for trouble to ignite. Joel noticed a couple of girls at the bar checking them out.

"Those girls keep looking at us," Joel said.

Derek barely glanced in their direction. "Let 'em keep looking."

"Man, when are you gonna come out of this? It's done, okay. At least we didn't get busted."

"But that's the thing, isn't it? I almost did get busted. That almost happened. And you didn't even stick around long enough to find out."

"What did you expect me to do?"

Derek shook his head at the floor. "I don't know. I don't know what the answer is."

"It's a risk, Derek. Don't you get that? It's dangerous. That's why we get paid."

"But we're not getting paid, are we?"

Joel threw up his hands. "If it'll shut you up I'll pay you myself."

"I don't want your money. Hell, I don't even know why I got involved in the first place." He faced Joel. "But what I really don't understand is how you could leave me like that. For all the stuff that could have happened, that was the last thing I would have guessed."

But the reason wasn't hard to understand at all. It was right there, hanging between them and had been all along. He'd panicked, sure, but beneath that was the fact that Joel was tired of waiting for Derek to catch up, and maybe there was even some small part of him that actually wanted Derek to get busted, let him see what it was like to fend for himself. They'd grown up under that same sad roof and Joel wasn't given anything to help him survive that Derek didn't get too, so why did it always fall on him to keep their lives in order?

"You know what'd be great?" Joel said. "If we could all look out for ourselves for a change."

Derek clucked his tongue and sulked off, parting the crowd with his size. At the bar the girls were still watching Joel. One of them pointed to the top of her head and waved him over. Joel glanced back at Derek.

"Damnit," he said. He downed the last of his beer and shouldered his way toward the girls.

"Let me see," one of them said. She reached up and grabbed a fistful of his hair. "It's soft."

She was nearly as tall as him, with dark, rheumy eyes from an early start of drinking. She had full lips and faint acne scars on her cheeks.

"Come on, Chief. You and your hair can buy us a drink."

She ordered some mixed shots and clapped her hands at the bartender as if to say hurry up. Joel asked for their names.

"What are our names tonight?" she asked her friend.

"Uh, she's Andrea and I'm Angela. That's our names."

"Whatever," Joel said.

"So let's see," Andrea said. "He's no student. You're not a student, right?"

"What gave me away?"

The bartender set the drinks in front of them, and when neither girl made a move he threw a few bills onto the bar.

She took his hand and held it nails-up for the other girl to see.

"These aren't the hands of a student," she said. "That much I know."

Angela held her chin. "I'm gonna say he grew up here. Did you? Are you a local boy?"

"No," Andrea said. "He's not local. Do you work in a machine shop?"

"Are we going to drink these or not?" Joel said.

Andrea ran her hand through his hair again, this time dragging her nails lightly along his scalp. "Come on, play with us. Tell us who's right."

"Construction," Joel said. "I live up in Langley."

Andrea pounded her fist on the bar. "Goddamnit I was close. Okay, let's drink."

"Wait," Angela said. "I bet he's got a kid."

They turned to Joel. "Do you?"

Joel shook his head. "You two need to back off."

Angela raised both arms above her head. "Yes! All me, girl!" she yelled into Andrea's face.

Andrea pounded the bar with both fists and one of the bartenders shouted at her over his shoulder.

"Oh, he's mad at us now. Don't be mad, Chiefie. We're sorry. Come on. Let's drink to your kid. What's his name?"

"Sam."

"All right, then," Angela said. "Let's drink to Sam. And to you, Chief. For being a good sport."

"Come on, Chiefie," Andrea said. "Come dance with me."

She took him by the wrists.

The music had changed from rock to a dance beat without him noticing. People were writhing in a small section in back.

"Not my thing," he said.

"Then make it your thing. Come on."

She pulled him through the crowd and began to grind against him. Joel did his best to keep up, not exactly dancing but moving with her body, pressing against her, resting his hands on her hips when she'd let him. After a while he'd had enough. His shirt was stuck to his back and he had a diamond of sweat in the center of his chest.

"How about we get another drink," he yelled over the music.

She grabbed him by the chin a little too rough. "No, dance with me, Chiefie."

She held his hands, and as he tried to get back in sync someone took her by the waist and swayed with her from behind. She leaned back against the guy and wrapped her arms around his neck.

Joel moved closer. "Hey, what's up?"

She smiled. "Hey, Chiefie," she said. "This is Chiefie."

"Hey, Chiefie," the guy said.

He had his face buried in the crook of her neck.

People danced around him as he considered his next move. He stared at the guy with the word nigger tumbling around his head, a word his father sometimes used when Joel was young, though not anymore. At some point his old man had become incensed by the possibility of being labeled a bigot. He bristled when they used terms like "hate crime" and "white privilege" in the news, argued that we'd come a long way and that no one was racist anymore, not really, and Joel figured he stopped using the word as proof that he wasn't, as if avoiding that single word made it so.

Joel had always been afraid of the word, the evisceration of it, but mostly because of the reaction it brought. He'd been in enough fights to know what you said mattered. Cut too deep and it could enrage the guy, make him unbeatable. The two were speaking close, swaying gently to the music. Joel found it hard to watch, as if he'd walked in on people fucking in a bathroom stall. With the music pulsing he looked around the room and snuck away.

At the bar he ordered another shot of vodka from a girl with tiny stars tattooed on the webs of her fingers.

"Hey, how about a real shot glass this time?" he said.

The girl shook her head. "We don't have any," she said. "Assholes keep stealing them."

From the way she set the plastic cup in front of him he figured she meant "assholes like you."

"Five fifty," she said, but Joel snatched his money off the bar before she could take it.

"Hold up." He threw back the shot and flicked the tiny plastic cup across the bar. "Let's do this again."

BUTTERFLIES

THEY HAD AGREED to meet at the fountain on campus. Francesca showed up late in a sweater with large white buttons up the front and dangly earrings that weren't quite gold or silver. Her perfume was sweet and reminded him of purple candy.

When Christopher had asked her out days before, she agreed only after a long stretch of silence that made him want to pedal back. It was never easy with her. He felt awkward whenever they were together, never quite sure if she truly enjoyed his company, and maybe that was what he found so attractive. He and Michele were friends first, the two of them silly, giggling classmates, teasing one another, using any excuse to touch. They had the same deep, romanticized love for dead musicians, artists like Buckley and Nick Drake, even mainstreamers like Cobain and Hendrix and Joplin, tragic figures whose early deaths somehow made them more appealing, perhaps because there was nothing more beautiful than what else they might have created. With Michele it was all so effortless.

Francesca was different. He was constantly analyzing everything she said, considering her facial expressions, the dip of her eyebrows in concentration. He found himself having to choose his words carefully so they didn't come out wrong, to time his responses so they wouldn't speak simultaneously. It was exhausting, but wasn't this how it should be? He'd been told his entire life that anything worthwhile had to be worked for, earned. Why would love be any different?

They ambled down the side streets towards Rich's place. The wind spun the leaves in tiny spirals on the grass, "witches dancing" they called it as kids. At the corner she stopped and removed one of her shoes, and when Christopher waited beside her she placed a hand on his shoulder and swiped something from the heel of her foot.

"What's your brother like?" she said.

"We get on okay. He's a bit older than me, but we always got along."

She slipped her shoe back on and they continued.

"I have a younger sister. Rebecca. We're nothing alike. We used to be close, but it's not like that anymore."

"What's different?"

"What's different?" she said, searching for an answer that seemed to elude her. "I guess I am. She's like my parents. They all have this idea of how life should be. I'm not like them."

He wanted to press but was afraid. She explained the details of her life as indifferently as if she were reading from a list of numbers, and all of it added up to the same end: she was alone. Christopher had yet to hear about someone she was close to.

As they came up on Rich's place the noise started to grow. He saw a few people sitting on the front stoop, their glowing cigarette coals hovering in the darkness. The back yard was done up with Christmas lights strung along the fence, those large bulbs you didn't see much anymore. A good number of them were out. The hole Rich had dug was covered over and a few people were standing on the oval of loose dirt.

"You want a beer?" Christopher said.

"I don't like beer," she said, which made Christopher feel like she didn't plan on staying long.

"I can get you something else."

"I'm fine."

Across the way Rich was talking to his roommate, Glen. Christopher raised a hand in the air, but Rich was already too far gone to notice.

He got a beer from the keg and managed to track down a bottle of red wine with an armadillo on the label. He filled a small plastic cup nearly to the brim and brought it to Francesca, who was sitting alone on a picnic bench. She took the wine as if she'd been waiting for it. He was about to sit beside her when Rich bear-hugged him from behind with such a running start it almost sent the two of them tumbling to the ground. Half his beer spilled over his wrist.

"Here's my brother," Rich said, still holding on, his chin poking over Christopher's shoulder.

Christopher introduced him to Francesca and Rich took a step back and nodded slightly.

"This here's Glen," Rich said as his roommate pulled alongside him.

Glen was impressive up close, rounded nearly from his chest to the bottom of his bloated groin. He was tugging on a Tiparillo, a can of Pepsi in his hand.

"Evening all," he said. He extended a hand to Christopher, then to Francesca. "Good to finally meet you."

Christopher recognized Glen from a picture he had seen on the refrigerator that first night in town. He was gliding across a Slip n' Slide on his enormous pink belly, grinning with a flash of straight white teeth. Within a few seconds Glen was telling them all about a weeklong run at online poker where he managed to pull in close to six hundred bucks, and he offered to show them the email receipts if they didn't believe him.

"It's all I do anymore," he said. "I log between twenty and thirty hours most weeks. At this point, I'm good enough to go head to head with guys who have been at it for years. That's the thing about the internet. Used to be you had to search for games with the best players in order to sharpen your skills. But now I can go online and find a game at any time, day or night. With professionals, too. It pisses off the old timers who've spent decades at the tables. Now you got guys in their twenties winning big money tournaments. I figure I got a shot in two or three more years."

"He's good," Rich said.

"Do you play at all?" Glen said.

Christopher shook his head. "I'm pretty terrible."

"We should play sometime. In less than an hour you'll know more about the game than most people."

"Isn't it hard to play online?" Christopher said. "You can't see anyone."

Glen poked at the air with his cigar. "That's the thing. You can still read your opponents. But since you can't see them you have to watch their moves. It helps you zero in on how they respond to each hand rather than the look on their face. Nobody at that level has a poker face. All that stuff about tells, that's Hollywood bullshit. Some guys even make up ticks to confuse you. You need to play the odds and respond to the moves of your opponent. That's it."

A girl sidled up to Glen and wrapped her arms around him, pressing her cheek against his chest. Glen lowered an arm onto her shoulder.

"This is Madeline," he said. "Not a bad card player in her own right."

Christopher wondered if they were a couple, and if so, how exactly that might work. Glen had at least a foot and two hundred pounds on her.

Madeline's nails were red with black dots like the backs of ladybugs. She had large gums and a streak of blond hair on the left side. On her feet were a pair of worn black Converse.

"We have games here on Sunday nights," Glen said. "You guys should sit in."

"I'm not playing cards with a bunch of ringers," Christopher said, and that got a laugh from Francesca.

"It does sound like fun, though," Francesca said.

At this, Madeline took both of her hands.

"And who are you?"

"Francesca. I'm a friend of Christopher's."

"How come I've never seen you before?"

"I haven't been here long. In Waylan, I mean."

"I love your barrettes."

Glen stamped out the Tiparillo on the bottom of his shoe and dropped it into the mouth of his Pepsi can.

"You need another beer or anything?" he asked Christopher. "We got other stuff inside if you want something with a little more bite."

"The keg is fine for me."

"How 'bout you, sister?"

Francesca blushed a little, something Christopher never imagined he'd see. "I'm okay."

Madeline stood on her toes and whispered something into Glen's ear. He thought for a moment and said, "Yeah, I guess that'd be okay."

She turned to Francesca, then to Christopher. There was excitement glistening in her eyes. "You guys want to see something cool?" she said.

Glen led them through the house. He opened the door to his bedroom and stood beside the threshold like an usher, and Francesca, Madeline, and Christopher filed inside. His room was immaculate. There were fresh vacuum lines in the carpet and the books on his shelf were arranged with the spines flush to the edge. A few were on poker: *Ace on the River, Every Hand Revealed.* The rest were textbooks and paperback novels. On the floor was a mattress that bowed in the center. It was carefully made, not a crease in the blue and gray quilt that stretched across the top. Glen closed the door as Madeline flopped down onto the bed. When Francesca saw this she took off her shoes and sat down, too.

Glen moved to a large glass tank in the corner. "So," he said, "this is Penelope. She's a reticulated python. I can't bring her out there because there are too many people, but you guys can have a look." He unclipped the mesh lid and leaned it carefully against the wall. "Everybody be cool. No big movements or anything. She can be temperamental."

He held the snake behind the head and lifted it out of the tank. Its skin was a pixilated honey-brown with white diamond patterns. Up close Christopher could see the narrow slits of its pupils.

"Can I?" Madeline said.

"Yeah, slowly. Don't take your eyes off her head."

"Is it poisonous?" Francesca said.

"No, but she has a serious set of teeth. You definitely don't want to get bit by her."

Madeline ran her fingers across the snake's back and shivered. She folded her arms across her chest and dropped back down next to Francesca, kicking her feet like a child overcome with excitement.

"You guys have to try it," she said.

Francesca laid her small, pale hand closer to Penelope's head than Christopher would have dared.

"That's it, go slow," Glen said.

"She's beautiful," Francesca said. "Look at those colors."

"Why get an animal like this?" Christopher asked. "It seems like a huge undertaking."

"It's a lot of work. I guess for me it's about being close to something you shouldn't be. That's a hell of a feeling. You have to make sure you don't get careless. I know someone who was bit on the cheek while feeding one of these guys, and he made the mistake of grabbing the head and pulling straight back. It's a natural reaction, but it's the last thing you want to do. The teeth are curved. What you need to do is slide them out the way they went in. Instead he tore out half his cheek and broke one of the fangs off inside. The left side of his face looks like hamburger now."

"Jesus," Christopher said.

"But the thing is, you can read them if you make the effort. I handle her a lot because it gets her used to people and also you get to know her better. Every animal has its own personality. I can tell when she's in a defensive pose or when she's getting agitated. There are things they do to warn you. You have to spot the signs."

He slid his hand up the snake's back to support her head more. "I can let one of you hold her, but that's it. She gets cranky. I don't want anyone getting hurt."

Francesca waved her hand in the air, supporting her arm at the elbow like a kid in grade school. "Oh me, Glen. Please let it be me."

ONCE PENELOPE was in her tank Glen led them back to the kitchen.

"You should wash your hands. Pythons carry small traces of Salmonella."

He squirted a dollop of dishwashing liquid onto each of their palms, then his own, and they squeezed in tight and lathered their hands under the running water.

"Time's up," Glen said, and he forced his body between Francesca and Madeline.

The two stumbled apart and Madeline swatted Glen on the chest, leaving a dark, sudsy handprint over his heart. It was clear they weren't a couple. There was love there, for sure, but it wasn't romantic love.

Outside Glen gathered a few stray folding chairs and set them up on the back lawn, one short of what was needed.

"What about you?" Francesca said.

"I'll collapse that thing," he said. "You guys go ahead. I'm more of a stander."

"Want a beer?" Christopher said. "I'm going that way."

"I don't drink," he said, and patted his stomach. "My vices lie elsewhere."

No one laughed with him. Glen seemed to have no trouble showing every part of himself, and what Christopher saw was a good guy doing himself in a little at a time, then making light of it, as if he had long ago resigned to his own worst inclinations.

Before it became uncomfortable Francesca leaned toward Madeline. "So, tell us about you," she said.

Madeline tucked her hair behind her ears. "Well, let's see. I'm finishing up a degree in Communication Design, but I like to work with watercolors. That's my real love."

"Check it out," Glen said. He pulled up his sleeve to expose a snake coiled around the upper part of his arm. "She designed the whole thing. It's only a few months old."

"It's amazing," Francesca said.

Madeline averted her eyes from the compliment. "I have a show on campus in a couple of weeks, and I'm all like ahhhhhh." She covered her face with both hands.

"November 4th and 5th," Glen said. "Save the date."

"I need to start going to things like that," Christopher said. "I didn't even know who Owen Turner was until a couple of weeks ago."

"It's true," Francesca said. "I had to bring him to the park."

Glen shook his empty Pepsi can. "I'm going for a refill."

"I'll go with you," Christopher said. "I'd like to talk to my brother while he's still able."

They found Rich at the kitchen table, eating a slice of pizza over a paper plate. Christopher and Glen grabbed seats on either side of him.

"How goes it, Rich?" Glen said.

"Doing okay." He looked at Christopher with an earnestness that didn't fit the moment. "You having a good time?"

"Yeah," Christopher said. "Hey, whatever happened to your pig roast?"

Rich had a jagged white crumb clinging to his lip, and he brushed it away with the back of his hand as if he'd right then caught a glimpse of himself.

"Oh, yeah. That was too much work."

"One of his fleeting moments of brilliance," Glen said.

Rich dropped the pizza crust onto the plate as if he couldn't take another bite. "You with that girl?"

Christopher glanced at the back door. "We met not too long ago. What about you? You guys got anything going on?"

Rich lifted his chin and scratched at the short brown hairs on his throat. He slapped a hand onto the back of Christopher's neck and squeezed.

"It's so damn good to have you here," he said.

By midnight, the crowd outside had thinned to about half. Christopher made his way slowly through the darkness to have a smoke. He smiled at the thought of Penelope draped over Francesca's shoulders, her body hunched forward from the weight, watching the snake's eyes so endearingly you'd think she'd raised the thing. It made sense that she'd hold her ground with a creature that could nearly swallow her whole, that she'd respect it could and look it dead in the eye, neither one of them the least bit frightened as long as that respect held.

She was sitting at the opposite side of the yard, beneath a cherry tree with crumbly gray bark that made it look diseased. She and Madeline had their chairs facing one another, close enough for their knees to touch. The two of them were leaned forward in the darkness, silent and still, their lips pressed and Madeline's ladybug fingers resting on Francesca's thigh.

"I MET THESE PEOPLE who were pretty cool," Rich said. "They'd been there a while, came out from North Carolina, or maybe Georgia. I can't remember."

They were stretched out on the living room sofas, listening to Rich ramble on about a camping trip he took to Yosemite two years ago. The story was going nowhere, but Christopher was content to listen. He was trying to hide without making it appear that way. At one point he put his head back on the sofa and shut his eyes, and when he opened them Francesca was standing over him. She held her elbows as if she were cold.

"Hey, I think I'm going to take off," she said.

"Okay," Christopher said.

Rich slapped him on the back as he stood.

Francesca gave a quick wave to Rich and Glen. "Thanks for letting me hold Penelope. It was really something."

"Come back and see her," Glen said.

She led the way outside and the two of them stood on the front porch facing one another, the space between them less than it had ever been.

"I can walk you back," Christopher said.

She turned and looked at the darkness behind her. "Madeline said she'd give us a ride." She pointed to a car idling a few houses down.

Christopher shifted his weight. "That's okay. I'm gonna hang out for a while."

She nodded, then sandwiched his hand between hers. Christopher flinched, surprised that she had made an effort to touch.

"I'll see you in class," she said, almost as a question.

"Absolutely."

She turned and headed down the steps right as Madeline switched on the headlights, and Christopher stood there on the porch until the car was gone.

Back inside he found Rich passed out with his head hanging forward. Glen stood at the kitchen sink getting water from the tap. He drained the glass in several large gulps and put it back under the faucet to fill it again.

"Need anything?"

"I'll grab one more beer," Christopher said, and before he could head out the back door Glen opened the refrigerator and pulled a bottle of Heineken out of the drawer meant for vegetables.

"Here, take the private stock. Your brother won't mind." He slid the bottle across the table. "The night treating you okay?"

Christopher nodded. "Everything's cool."

Glen tore off a square of paper towel and wiped down his face.

"I was with this girl not too long ago," he said, as if to answer the question Christopher had asked earlier. "Karen. She dumped me at the Bronx Zoo. You ever been there?"

Christopher shook his head.

"As far as zoos go, it's okay. Good but not great. I mean, they do a nice job with the layout and they have some amazing habitats for the animals, but they don't have much of a reptile exhibit. But it's such a trip to see animals in the middle of the Bronx. I mean, the parkway is literally a stone's throw away, and you have all these animals oblivious to that. I have a picture of this huge field with about ten enormous buffalo standing around, going about their business. It's surrounded by trees and looks like you're somewhere in the country, but if you look up you can see an office building poking its head above the treetops. I always wondered what it must be like for people on the top floors. Imagine looking out your window to see Prospect Avenue in one direction and a herd of buffalo in the other. But the coolest part is their butterfly exhibit. It's this small hut kind of thing, maybe the size of our living room. For a couple of bucks you can watch the butterflies all around you. Karen didn't want to go in, but I talked her into it. So we go and they're in these little trees and fluttering through the air and once in a while they'll land on you. Hundreds of them. It's pretty incredible. I mean, if you think about it, at no other time in history would you find all those different butterflies in the same place. I don't know. I think it's cool. Anyway, we're standing there and Karen tells me it's over. So she's there feeling horrible and I'm all depressed and it's raining fucking butterflies."

He tipped back his head to laugh big enough to show his back teeth.

Christopher started to laugh too, and the two of them got lost in it. "She ever say why?"

"It was time to move on, I guess. But those butterflies, man. It's something I'll never forget. I mean, yeah, I was dumped, but talk about your silver linings."

He drummed on the table with his fingertips and looked around the place.

"We'll be cleaning this shithole all day tomorrow. You should come by. We'll throw some burgers on the grill. Maybe play a few hands."

"I might be up for that," Christopher said, and he balanced on the back legs of his chair like he were floating.

BETWEEN WORLDS

J OEL WASN'T READY to go when the lights came up. Over the past hour he'd recharged and now he was ready to take that feeling somewhere else. The girl he'd danced with was gone, along with that asshole who cock-blocked him. They had slipped out without him noticing and now he felt like someone was pumping waves of electricity into his bloodstream. He'd been caught on his heels earlier, unsure how to react to a guy who barely seemed to notice him standing there, but if he saw him now he wouldn't be able to keep from getting in the guy's face and seeing it through.

Beside him a girl was saying goodbye to a small group of people. She placed a hand on the back of an empty chair while her friends paid their tabs. Joel noticed a dull silver ring on her finger, the setting a polished oval of turquoise. He pressed on the stone like a button and she snatched back her hand. She covered the ring and mumbled something he couldn't make out, and her girlfriend put an arm on her back and shuffled her towards the exit with the rest of the group.

"Good talking to you," he said for Derek's benefit, who was leaning against the bar like it was the only thing holding him up.

"We need to find Marcus," Derek said.

"Yeah, where is that little prick?"

"I'll get him."

"Tell him, 'While we're young.'"

Derek walked across the room like a grizzly on its hind legs. Moments later he came back with Marcus following a few paces behind. He had a pink Hawaiian lei around his neck.

"Where'd you get that?" Joel said.

Marcus looked down at his chest. "Let's hit the diner on the way home. I'm starving."

Joel pushed away the last of his beer. "All right, let's get the hell out of here."

Outside, the fresh air was a jolt. Joel took in a breath and had to wait out a wave dizziness that tilted everything to the left and slowly leveled off. A couple of girls moved past them, leaving behind a trail of soapy perfume. Marcus removed the lei and tried to place it over the head of one of them. She ducked away before he could make it happen.

"Whoa, whoa," Joel called after her. "Don't be mad."

One of the girls said fuck you over her shoulder and they made their way back to the car with Marcus imitating the mousy tone of her voice. Joel decided to have one last cigarette before getting in. Before he could get his lighter to catch he heard someone shout in his direction. He lifted his eyes slowly.

"Great," Marcus said. "Now we're never getting out of here."

He and Derek were already coming around the car, their shoulders dropped as if this had messed up their plans.

Joel crushed the cigarette in his hand and let it fall to the ground.

"What was that?" he called. "I didn't hear you."

Three guys were standing at the edge of the parking lot, and Joel could see that two of them wanted no part of what was coming. They had their hands in their pockets, elbows tucked close to their sides. It was the third guy who had taken the lead, standing under the streetlight in a tight T-shirt and jeans with slits at the knees, his face so smooth it made him look like a giant baby.

"I like the hairdo," he said. "Seriously. It's very pretty."

Joel approached them slowly, leaving a few extra feet of space. "There a problem? Because I'd love to hear about it."

Big Baby was grinning. "What'd you say to those girls?"

Joel looked back in their direction. "What's that got to do with you?"

"I've been listening to you run your mouth all fucking night," Big Baby said. "This little fuck, too."

Marcus put a hand to his chest as if to say "me?"

Joel chuckled to himself for show. "Come on, man. You're kidding me, right?"

"You losers come into our house with that stupid fucking hairdo and start shit all night? Who the fuck do you think you are?"

"Look little boy, you're in way over your head. You understand?"

Big Baby puckered his lips like a kiss, and that sent a mild shiver through Joel's body. The guy had been gearing up for a while. Now he'd gotten himself to a place where nothing would bring him back. From the size of him Joel figured he was going to take as much damage as he'd give, and if he wasn't careful he might come out on the losing end of this. The guy came forward a little and Joel wasn't able to stop himself from taking a step back.

Something yipped a few feet behind them and they all turned to find a squad car slowing to a stop.

"Stay right there," the officer said through a loudspeaker, though no one had tried to leave.

Joel kept his eyes on Big Baby, who was smiling at him. When the officer finally made his way over he found a place between them, spotting right away where the tension was strongest.

"Let's see some I.D.s, fellas." He collected them one at a time, holding them under a Maglite before handing them back. "What's the problem?"

Big Baby sucked air through his bottom teeth. "No problem, officer," he said.

"You all students?"

"No," Joel said, and the cop looked him over.

Then he turned to Big Baby and asked them where they were headed and one of the guys pointed towards the university.

"Then why don't you get moving," he said.

They set off up the hill, Big Baby glancing back a few times, blowing another kiss, jutting his shoulders forward as if to make Joel flinch again.

"Where are you guys coming from?" the cop said, still holding Joel's license.

"Langley," Joel said.

"You came all the way out from Langley?"

"It's my birthday," Derek said, and the cop threw him a look that said he'd talked out of turn.

"I suggest you get to wherever it is you need to go." He handed Joel back his license with two fingers. "Understand? I don't want to see you the rest of the night."

Marcus and Derek started towards the car, but Joel didn't move. He put his license back into his wallet and watched the officer.

"There something else you want?" the cop said.

"No," Joel said. "I'm good," and he walked away fighting every impulse he had.

INSIDE THE CAR it was quiet enough for Joel to hear the vinyl seat squawking beneath his weight. He tried to make the traffic light and had to slam on the breaks at the last second.

"Let's go find them," he said.

"Bad idea," Marcus said. "The cops are out, man. You're gonna get a D.U.I."

"Fuck it. Let's finish this."

"Let it go, Joel. I need a goddamn cheeseburger. I'm dying back here."

"Yeah," Derek said. He had his head against the window like he was about to go to sleep. "Let's go home already."

"You guys are pussies, you know that?"

"Yeah, I know," Marcus said. "I came to terms with that a long time ago." He reached over the console and pointed through the windshield. "Stop at that store real quick. My mouth tastes like sawdust."

Joel swung to the curb and told Marcus to hurry the fuck up. He could still see Big Baby smiling at him with that same look everyone in this town seemed to have, like they dismissed him, like he didn't matter. He watched a couple of girls coming up the sidewalk, walking arm in arm and sharing a cigarette. At the corner another girl was showing off with a hula hoop. It moved up and down her body, and at one point she brought it all the way to her neck. Joel had come here to feel the weight of what he could have had, to gauge his level of regret. Instead he found yet another life he wanted no part of, which left him only with the life he had now, and that was never going to be enough. He didn't belong in either world, this one or his own. He was somewhere in between them both, and watching these people take to their lives so well made him want to burn the entire place to the ground.

The girl with the hula hoop was still at it, and as he watched a kid came around the corner and had to step into the street to avoid bumping into her. He was holding a cell phone, not smiling but happy, it seemed. Joel recognized the long, skinny arms, the moppy hair. It was the kid from the park, the one who'd bummed a smoke off him. He thought about the girl with him that day and how she wasn't with him now and he wondered if it was her on the phone. It made the hair stand on his arms because of all the options this kid had and how he got to live a life that suited him and how he probably didn't even realize what he had, this goddamn kid, and suddenly Joel was out of the car and moving towards him.

"Hey, who you talking to?" he called.

The kid slowed, maybe expecting to see someone he recognized. And then he averted his eyes and started walking again.

"I'm not talking to you," he said.

Joel headed him off. He snatched the cell phone from his hand and threw it across the street.

"What?" he said. "What the fuck did you say?"

He could feel momentum pulling him along, guiding him in a single direction like running downhill.

The kid's eyes went wide because he knew what was coming, even if he didn't know why, and he said "hold on" like Joel didn't know what he was doing.

Joel landed a fist on the side of the kid's head, dropping him to the pavement, hard and shoulder-first like someone had swept his legs. His eyes rolled and he covered his head to refocus and looked up at Joel like this was all a mistake, like he could explain if Joel would give him the chance. But Joel wasn't going to give him that chance, because now it was his turn to show this kid a life, his life, and he reached back and brought it all down with him.

GROUND

DEREK HAD pulled him towards the car. He remembered that. And also Marcus standing outside the convenience store with an open bag of chips.

"Get in," Derek had said, the rising panic giving him trouble with the door handle. Joel threw the car into gear and swung onto the road. He flew down one of the side streets towards the highway, and when he jumped onto Route 211 a police cruiser was waiting for him. Off in the distance he could hear more on the way.

None of them had said a word in the squad car, but now, at the police station, hands cuffed behind their backs, crammed into a bench that wasn't wide enough for the three of them, Marcus was laughing.

"Jesus. I think that kid was on the ground before you hit him."

It was over. Joel had finally done himself in. He'd been working his way towards this point and now he was calm because it couldn't get any worse. There would be another court date and another strike against him and Lynn would be secure in the fact that she was right about him all along. There wasn't much more he could do to fuck things up. He'd finally hit bottom, and with the ground under him maybe he could find enough footing to start climbing his way back to a better life.

"How long they gonna keep us, you think?" Derek said.

"It'll fall on me," Joel said. "You'll be okay."

Marcus let his head drop back against the wall. "Why'd you have to do this shit, Joel? We're going to be here all night."

The gleaming floor tiles reminded Joel of a hospital, where that kid was probably being patched up now. The officer who had brought them in was seated at a desk nearby, typing on his computer using only his index fingers. Then the phone on his desk lit up and he answered and listened for a while and his eyes went wide and leveled on the three of them. He hung up the phone and ducked into another room. Marcus and Derek didn't seem to notice that something had changed. The officer came back with two others and there was an urgency that wasn't there before. One of them took Joel hard by the elbow and walked him down the corridor. He turned to see Derek and Marcus being pulled in the opposite direction.

"What's going on," Joel said.

"Come with me," the officer said.

"Where are you taking me?"

"Keep moving," he said.

The guy kept his eyes straight ahead, as if he couldn't bring himself to look at Joel at all. They stopped at a security door and the officer waited for someone to buzz them in, and when they reached a small holding cell the officer opened the door and put him inside.

"Come on," Joel said. "Tell me what's going on."

The officer flexed his jaw in a way that said he'd give anything for five minutes alone with Joel in that cell. Anything.

"That boy you beat. He's dead."

And then the door shut with a loud clatter and Joel was alone.

WALK HOME

WHEN HE LEFT Rich's place, the sky was equal parts western and horror film. It was clear mostly, with a wide plane of clouds rippling across the horizon, overextending itself so that soon it would dissolve entirely. Christopher imagined sleeping right there on someone's lawn, curled up on his side like a cowboy out on a great expanse of the south west, the campfire burning until he eased into sleep. Yet that same stretch of cloud seemed to be moving in with a purpose, heading toward the waning moon as if to snuff it out entirely so the world could release what hid in its darkest places.

He had no need for sleep, not now. Standing beneath the porch light with Francesca had released him of the awkwardness he'd been wrestling with for weeks, and being free from that energized him. He'd gotten a glimpse of who they were with their guards down. On Monday he would wave without worrying about what it would mean and that would be that. What he wanted now was to be close to her the way Glen was close to Madeline, so that a few years from now they could hold desperately onto one another at graduation, the two of them in maroon and gold robes, clinging to their friendship. And then later maintaining that connection while their lives moved in different directions, both of them secure in the fact that they always had one another to turn to. He wanted to tell her about Michele and what they'd once had and how he missed her more than he had expected. He wanted to hear what she thought about it all, but mostly he wanted her to listen and to know him, to share with her that part of his life.

The last time he'd slept with Michele—lying on the tight nylon carpeting of her basement, her parents sleeping two floors above—she had watched his eyes the entire time, touching his face with her fingertips and barely making a sound, as if she had shut down her body so she could concentrate entirely on him.

If he left now he could be in Pittsburgh by dawn. Then he could call her and say, "Look out your window," and he'd be standing there, alone in the parking lot outside her dorm, lifting his hand on the hope that she might come down and let him in. He could see it clearly. And if she became angry that he had taken such liberties, so what? The risk excited him almost as much seeing her, maybe more, because doing nothing when he wanted her so badly seemed like a waste of his own life, and he didn't want to waste another second.

He dug into his pocket for his phone and started dialing. In the distance a dog was barking, and he veered off the sidewalk and steadied a course down the center of the road, which stretched before him like a calm, dark river, bending toward the university. A block away he could see cars bottlenecked at the Quick Stop on Main Street. The bars had just let out, he realized, and people were moving in swarms. At the corner he could see a girl working a hula hoop. Her body churned with the serpentine movements of a belly dancer, and the hoop hovered there, free from gravity, orbiting around her waist.

Shawn picked up after a few rings. There was music in the background and Christopher could hear him talking to Haley before saying hello.

"You awake?" Christopher said.

"Yes I am. What's on your mind?"

"Any chance I could borrow your car? Like tonight."

"Tonight? You and that girl running away together?"

"I thought I'd take a ride to Pitt. As a surprise."

"That so," Shawn said, and Christopher could hear him talking to Haley again. When he came back on the line he said, "You're a goddamn romantic is what you are."

The girl with the hula hoop was only a few feet away, and he stopped right there in the road to watch her. She worked the hoop up to her chest and over her shoulders and turned it around her slender neck, then threaded her arms through and brought it back down to her hips. He found it all so sensual, and he clapped awkwardly with his phone still in his hand. As he moved away from the tranquil side-streets and towards the bright, busy intersection on Main, it was like swimming up from the bottom of a lake, leaving behind the quiet and heading towards the light and sound and movement that lay beyond the water's surface. And glancing once over his shoulder to see where he'd been, he took the corner and headed out.

HEADLINES

I T WAS ARLENE'S SISTER, Barbara, who always grabbed the reins in times of crisis. She'd handled the arrangements for both of their parents years ago, from treatments to nursing homes to hospice, managing every painful and inconvenient detail with the steadiness of an emergency room worker. Years ago she sent Arlene a check each month after Jack had left (a hundred dollars here and there, whatever she could do), and she helped with the boys whenever she could. She was at her best taking charge when no one else wanted to. And with the phone ringing every half hour—calls from reporters, relatives she hadn't heard from in years, co-workers—Barbara came to stay with Arlene until things leveled off again.

From her spot on the sofa, where she'd been for most of the past two days, even to sleep (her bedroom felt so cold), Arlene could hear Barbara handling the phone throughout the day, telling callers the family had no comment so diplomatically you'd think she'd trained for this her entire life.

Only once did Arlene hear her break from the script, saying with a rise in her voice, "These boys. These are good boys," then slamming down the receiver.

Arlene first heard what had happened from the local news, and for the life of her she couldn't understand how they could have made such a mistake. They mentioned her sons by name, but her boys were upstairs sleeping off their night out, not in custody as the newscaster had said. She remembered hearing them come in late, lumbering with heavy steps up the stairs and into their bedrooms. Joel already had enough going on in his life. News like this, regardless of how untrue, might be the final shove to a family already teetering on the edge. She worried that people wouldn't tune in to hear the retraction once the media realized Joel and Derek had been mistaken for other boys, for violent criminals. She stayed on the couch until late that morning, waiting for them to come downstairs, holding on to her anger because releasing it might reveal something she wasn't willing to consider. She ignored the phone ringing in the kitchen, and by early afternoon, with her bladder painfully full and her joints aching from holding the same rigid position, Arlene heard Barbara let herself in the front door. She stood frozen in the entryway, taking long, stammering breaths.

"I swear I heard them last night," Arlene told her. "I swear."

Arlene listened to the fading shriek of the tea kettle as Barbara removed it from the burner. A few minutes later she came into the living room with two large mugs.

"Did you sleep at all?" she said.

"Towards the morning a little."

"We can get something from your doctor. Antidepressants maybe. Or at least something to help you sleep. I'll give her a call today."

She eased herself into the rocking chair in the corner.

"I don't want drugs," Arlene said.

"Half the country takes that stuff to get through a normal day, Arlene. There's nothing wrong with a little help at a time like this."

"The last thing I want is to feel better. Feeling good would make it worse."

"It would help you get by for a little while," Barbara said. Her bracelets jangled as she set the mug on the end table. "But I understand what you mean."

Arlene wanted to call the boy's parents, but Barbara had stopped her.

"What can you possibly say?" she'd said.

Arlene didn't have an answer. What she wanted was to listen, let them scream at her, release the pain they'd been feeling. If only she could shoulder at least some small part of their grief so they could feel a little less empty when they first opened their eyes each morning.

"All those kids who saw it happen," Arlene said. "Why didn't they do something? They could have stopped it. Couldn't they have stopped it?"

She kept tripping over this thought, aware that she was expecting others to save the world from her son.

Barbara rested her hands on the crest of her belly and clasped her fingers. She'd had her nails done recently, a smoky maroon color that made her look overdressed in the daylight. She sat calmly, waiting out one of Arlene's most recent spells.

"You have to cry at some point, Arlene. You can't keep torturing yourself."

She hadn't the slightest urge to cry. Not once. She had shut down early that first morning and now she was floating in a bubble where nothing could touch her. She wasn't afraid anymore. Life had delivered its worst. That's why she couldn't bring herself to see her boys. Not yet. It would reveal to her in the cruelest of ways that all her years as a mother had come to this, that she had raised two boys only to watch them meet the worst possible end. It seemed that the world would have been better off had she never been a mother at all. A horrible thought, but it was true, wasn't it? For two days she combed through Joel's life, tracing the line backwards to find the moment that set him off course and changed him from her son to a murderer. As if it were a single mistake, her mistake.

The doorbell gave Arlene a start. Barbara gripped the armrests and pulled herself out of the chair. She went to the window and parted the blinds with her fingers.

"It's Lynn," she said.

Arlene shook her head. "I can't see her now."

"Maybe you should. It might be good for you both."

"Is my grandson with her?"

"No, she's alone."

Arlene thought a moment. "Okay, then."

Barbara opened the door and stood looking out. Without a word she raised a hand to ask Lynn inside.

"I'll bring you some tea," she said.

Lynn seemed to be working up the courage to come inside. She shut the door behind her and settled down beside Arlene. It had been months since Arlene had seen her, the last time when she brought Sam for a visit on Easter morning. Arlene liked to put together a basket for him every year: chocolate eggs and Marshmallow Peeps and bubbles, a few pristine gold dollars she'd get from the bank. It was an hour-long visit that felt like it was timed to the second while Lynn was on her way to someplace else.

Now Lynn was dressed in work clothes, a pencil skirt that was too short and a simple white blouse, a pair of tattered black flats that made her look frumpy. She was forever the unruly teenager who didn't completely understand professional attire.

"I've been worried about you," Lynn said. "I can't imagine what you're going through right now."

Arlene was surprised by her empathy. Lynn had grown up in the valley, where compassion always seemed a hair off from the rest of the world.

"Probably the same as you," she said.

"It's hard to face people. At work no one will look me in the eye. It's like they don't know how to feel. About any of it. About me."

"They're as shocked as we are. But right now your concerns lie elsewhere." She said this with an unintended firmness she didn't regret. "Do you understand?"

Lynn nodded. "I don't know what to tell him. How do I explain something like this to a little boy? I don't get it myself. I don't."

"I'm sure he knows something's up. Maybe sit him down and talk to him as best you can."

Lynn looked toward the window, where bars of sunlight were coming through the blinds.

"I wish we could leave," she said. "Like today. Just grab what we need and get as far away from this as possible. It could buy me some time, a couple of years before I'd have to help him through it. Maybe that could make a difference."

She uncrossed her legs and held her knees together so that her heels splayed like a little girl wrestling with a Sunday dress.

"Can you believe I'm not angry? I know I should be, but I'm not. For once I'm not. I just want Sam to be okay. That was the first thing I thought of when I found out. I feel like it's the most important thing I've ever had to do."

"So far you've gotten it right when it comes to that little boy. This'll be no different."

Lynn wilted at these words, under the release of hearing that, in the eyes of someone else, she was a good mother.

"Do you think it happened because of me?" Lynn said. "Because we were moving? He was having such a hard time with it."

"Honey—"

Lynn slid down off the couch and onto the floor and lay her head on Arlene's lap. "I'm scared for him. I shouldn't be but I am."

Arlene held her hands in the air a moment before letting them rest in the girl's hair.

WITHDRAWAL

H E CALLED HIS MOTHER that first morning, nauseated and dizzy from a hangover and lack of sleep and the sobering jolt of where he was. They set him up in a small room with a couple of tables and a phone on each one, and he hunched forward and cupped his hands around the receiver as it rang. His mother never picked up, and after that first call he stopped trying. There was nothing she could do, and he was afraid hearing her break down on the line would loosen some part of him he might never recover.

The next day they brought him to a different facility. In the afternoon they led him to a visiting area where two other inmates were already seated, guys with wide backs and thick arms, one guy's head shaved clean with a cross tattooed on the back of his skull. He expected his mother to be waiting for him, but when he saw his dad he wasn't disappointed. If not for the glass he would have thrown his arms around him and held on tight.

His father looked like a man days from dying in his sleep, disappearing from this life without any fight at all. His cheeks were sunken and a heavy waddle of flesh sagged beneath his chin. In the corners of his mouth were calcified stains of dried spittle. They picked up the receivers at the same time and Joel watched his father's veiny blue lip quiver.

"You okay?" his father said.

Joel looked into his father's runny yellow eyes and nodded. He still had trouble responding to questions. His mind worked slower in here. Whenever someone spoke he had to repeat the words in his head, like rereading a paragraph in a book he didn't understand.

"What—" his father said and abandoned the thought. "Some guys at work read about it on the computer. They asked if it was any relation. That's how I found out." He lowered his head so Joel could barely see his face. "I had to tell them it was my son."

Joel squeezed his eyes tight to keep it together.

His father took in a breath and exhaled a little calmer. "If I'd been near the ocean right then I would have walked in and never come out."

"Dad," Joel said.

"I called your mother, but she wouldn't get on the phone. I talked to your Aunt Barbara. It's like this whole goddamn world is coming apart. You kids killing one another over nothing."

"It's not what you think," Joel said.

His father's eyes drifted to the ceiling. "It's not what I think," he whispered.

"It was a mistake. I never meant for this."

"And your brother," he said. "Jesus Christ."

"Is he okay?"

"I haven't had the nerve to see him yet. He's not made like you, Joel. He won't last in a place like this. I don't see how he could." His father moved the phone to his other ear. "They let that other boy go. Your friend."

"He had nothing to do with it," Joel said.

Marcus never would have thrown a punch, and if only he'd gotten outside sooner he might have been able to keep Joel from coming unhinged. Derek, too. When Joel first spoke to the police he'd told them Derek wasn't involved because that's what he remembered, but the images had been unfolding ever since: flashes of Derek standing over the kid, taking his boot to the kid's body.

"You talk to a lawyer yet?"

Joel nodded. "I'm scared, Dad. They're throwing everything

at us." He pressed his forehead hard against the glass. "Christ, it was only a fight. It started happening and I couldn't stop it."

He only partly believed this. Something had come over him that was difficult to control, but it was his doing. He'd worked himself into a wave of anger and went with it, let it take him like an ocean current, but all along he had it in him to move frantically against the tide and he didn't.

His father was hunched forward, both elbows on the table and the phone barely resting against his ear.

"It's all so pointless, Joel. How could it come to this?"

"I know guys who are involved in robberies," Joel said. "I can give names. Whatever they need."

His father blinked with confusion. "What are you talking about?"

"Criminals. I can testify against them."

"I don't understand. What good would that do?"

"Maybe I can get a deal. Some kind of leniency."

His father dropped back in his chair. "Son, don't you understand how serious this is? I mean, don't you get it?"

"I have to do something. They think I'm a murderer."

His father leaned closer to the glass. "Christ, Joel. Don't you see?"

ISAAC

IN HIS CART and the horse lurching up the road on such a pleasant day, another gift, this day, the sun and the autumn breeze, and the traffic whipping past him, worse now with the school in session than it had been during the summer, radios blaring as cars flash by, but his horse still steady, a good horse all these years, not prone to distraction, through the back roads alongside the park where the curves make it hard to see, and one car behind him getting impatient, he can tell, leaning to the left to try and pass, then accelerating once there is enough straight road, pushing it a little out of frustration, and the other cars following his lead, flashing by Isaac one after another.

He is alone today and he misses having Hannah beside him, his eldest, helping with deliveries. He could use her help. His leg is tight at the knee. It has slowed him all morning. Hannah bringing the quilts and watching little Sarah besides, Hannah who is approaching sixteen and how it unnerves him, getting so close to being a woman, and always that glow to her, much like Mirium, that yearning for more that seems to shine from behind her eyes. And the way Mirium defends their daughter because she knows where it comes from, from Mirium herself, something deep within her that lured Isaac from the beginning, that beautiful light inside her. How Mirium shied from him at first, playing with the idea of living with the English, living away from her family and her faith, and now Hannah with that same look of being held in place, not against her will, exactly, but something else, something inside pushing her along, telling her to go, a voice in her ear. He does not like to think about whose voice it is, talking and talking as it still seems to with Mirium at times, overtaking her during prayer, her body twitching while she wrestles with Lord knows what, with leaving him, it seems, though he never truly believes that. But now Hannah, so young and sweet and beautiful, the thought of not seeing her if she ever does leave (how could he shun her, his own daughter?), no longer able to speak to her or watch her read at night by the fire, so engrossed in books she is, so smart, and the way she makes them all laugh in the evenings, imitating her brothers, their slouching gaits and fluttering voices, teasing. The way she looks at the students whenever they ride past the school, wondering what she's thinking.

He is an able man but he cannot protect Hannah from the English world. It is too big. He worries for her and perhaps equally for himself, for the possibility of losing her. Mirium saying she could never shun if it came to that, but what choice is there? How could they release their daughter into the English world and still allow her a place in their hearts? People would object, the elders especially. So much danger in this town alone, so close now with that boy who was killed right down the road, the anger in young people, with no cause besides. He doesn't like to focus on the bad parts of the English world. There is good out there, he knows, kind, loving people, good Christians, people who love and care for their children, no different from Isaac's world, but a lack of control, an inability to keep the bad things away, too big, their world, too complicated, too many people to concern themselves with, and the thought of Hannah being among them, so vulnerable, his fears when the English boys call to her as they ride through town, such horrible words for young boys, such anger. Where does it come from?

And anger in himself now, he is ashamed to admit, every time he thinks of those boys, hurting for the sake of hurting, wanting someone else to feel the same pain as them. Such an ache he feels for that boy who was stricken, in one instant young and strong, in the next gone, the turn in one's life so fast and severe it seems impossible, the thought of that boy's family getting the news. Isaac has felt anger for days, burning deep inside him, even after he prayed and prayed, laying it at the feet of the Lord, yet the anger still lodged in his spine. It will take time, as with everything else, but the Lord will deliver. If only he could teach those boys the same, the boys that beat the life from that young man. He could show them, explain that they didn't have to succumb to anger, how they could give it away, hand it back to the Lord and in return take on His love and His work, such a fair trade. The anger is too much for one person, but not with the Lord's help. Isaac is not certain he could ever convince those boys, but in time he maybe could embrace them in his own heart, set aside his own anger and love them, in time, whether they want him to or not, and Hannah too if she ever chose to leave, the need for the English world more to her than family, than her relationship with the Lord. It seems impossible to him now, but perhaps in time, with the help of the Lord he could overcome the anger inside him, bring himself to hold out his arms and embrace all these children, every one of them, the good and the misguided and the tempted, and say again and again to convince even himself: You are forgiven.

RESPECTS

I F SHE DIDN'T know better Arlene would have thought snow was on the way. There were still leaves on the trees, brittle and curled and trembling on the branches, but the light around her was a winter blue and she could smell moisture in the air with a mix of fireplace smoke and fresh soil. It was too warm for snow, but not by much. Winter was coming in hard and people seemed to take notice. It wasn't even Thanksgiving and already one of the houses had Christmas lights coiled around the banisters with glinting streams of garland.

She'd been in her car for a while, watching the woman rake leaves into a neat pile and bear-hug them into one of those tall paper bags. Moments ago she had leaned the rake against a tree and disappeared inside the house, and Arlene wondered if she'd seen enough to afford herself a few more hours sleep at night. If that were true she could start the car and head home a little better off.

As a hard wind rolled over the neighborhood the woman came out of the house again, this time wearing a puffy orange vest and a pair of gardening gloves. She took up the rake, and as she did she looked right at Arlene, squinting with curiosity at the car parked a short distance from her home. Arlene did her best to not look threatening. She fiddled with the radio and rummaged through the glove compartment, and when she looked again the woman was coming towards her. Arlene braced herself. She lowered the window and smiled.

"Hi," the woman said. "Is everything okay?"

"I think I got a little off course. I'm sorry to disturb you."

"Where are you trying to go?"

"If you can point me back to 76, I can make it the rest of the way."

The woman looked in the direction Arlene had driven in. "It's a little tricky from here. I can write it down."

"It's fine," Arlene said. She worked the key into the ignition. "I'm sure I can figure it out."

"It's no problem," the woman said, and she walked towards the house as if the matter were settled.

Arlene thought about pulling away. Instead she exited the car and followed the woman across the lawn, where the leaves skittered by on their points. The woman held open the door. When Arlene went inside the warmth snatched her breath, a dry heat like when you open the oven. There was a wood burning stove in the corner and the change in temperature formed little pricks of sweat on her back and up her arms.

"Let me grab a pen," the woman said.

Arlene lingered near the door and unhooked the top buttons of her coat. It was every bit the kind of home she had imagined, small and modest, provincial. She figured the living room wasn't a place where anyone spent a lot of time. There was a loveseat and a couple of armchairs and a spinet piano against the wall, but it had the feel of an office lobby, a waiting room for guests like herself.

On the mantle was the boy's picture, his head tilted and lips parted as if he were about to speak. Arlene had seen him in the newspapers. She had first expected someone more threatening, weathered and rough-edged like her own boys, not this smooth-skinned young man. It was hard to understand how a boy like this could ignite such rage in her son. Beside his picture were votive candles that had burned themselves down to the metal discs.

Arlene sensed someone in the room, and she turned to find a man standing behind her. He had the sad blue eyes of a Husky. There were dark creases in his clothes as if he'd slept in them.

"You here to talk to my mother?" he said.

Arlene hugged herself around the middle. "I was outside," she said.

He scratched at his beard. "I can talk to you now. I couldn't before, but now I can."

"I'm sorry," Arlene said. "I don't think—"

"It was hard when you people first showed up," he said. He looked around the room. "I'm afraid this is gonna go away. Like it never happened. I can't imagine anything worse."

Before Arlene could speak the woman entered the room and laid a hand on the man's shoulder.

"It's okay, Richard," she said. "She came in for directions. That's all."

Richard stepped closer to Arlene and shook his head.

"Oh," he said. "I thought you were someone else." And with that he turned and left the room.

The woman watched the empty space where he'd been standing.

"My son," she said. "I'm not used to having him home. You'll have to excuse us. Our family has been through a lot recently."

She looked at the scrap of paper in her hand and held it out to Arlene.

"There's a fork at the bottom of this hill. You'll need to keep left or you're going to get confused. I'm Sheila, by the way. I'm sorry, I didn't get your name."

"Arlene."

She stuffed the slip of paper into her coat pocket and turned towards the door, but Sheila didn't make a move. She watched Arlene thoughtfully, with kindness.

"Arlene," she said. "You're here because of Christopher, aren't you?"

Another rush of heat moved up through Arlene's body. Her arms and legs pulsed. She tried to speak and swallowed the effort, and finally she said, "I shouldn't have come."

"It's okay," Sheila said. She moved Arlene towards the sofa. "It's okay. Here, sit a moment."

They sat close and Arlene took a breath. "I've been wanting to come for a long time. I don't know what to say. What is there to say?"

"Lots of people have come to pay their respects," Sheila said. "I know it comes from a place of love." She fiddled with the zipper on her jacket. "You know, I wouldn't let him play football. Can you believe that? Things like that sound so ridiculous to me now. I used to give him such a hard time about smoking. He would never do it around me, but I could smell it on his clothes. I feel like I was afraid of the wrong things, fighting the wrong battles. But how can you tell the difference between one concern and another when they all are so frightening? How can we know?"

"Yes," Arlene said.

"And even if we did know, what could be done? It's not fair that we can't control such things. Even if we do everything right." She pulled a crumpled tissue from beneath her sleeve and dabbed her nose. "It's easy to feel alone in this. Like we did something wrong, my husband and I. Why was it our child and no one else's, right? What was our mistake?" She sniffed and cleared her throat. "Funny. You'd think it was Richard who gave me these gray hairs, but Christopher was the one I always worried about. It was a feeling with him. Like I had to be extra careful. It was like I always knew. My husband has begun to question his faith. I've been trying not to think that way. But why give him to us only to take him away? What possible good could come from that?"

"Yes," Arlene whispered.

Sheila breathed deeply and tucked the tissue back under her sleeve and appeared renewed, as though she had learned how to turn off her grief and set it aside for another time. She smiled and rubbed small circles on Arlene's back.

"So, tell me, Arlene, how did you know my son?"

Arlene covered her mouth. She took Sheila's hands and held them tight and shut her eyes. When she opened them Sheila was waiting patiently for Arlene to collect herself.

She said, "I'm Arlene. My son. My son is Joel Martin."

Sheila leaned closer and nodded and then her eyes changed. She shook her head and tried to withdraw.

But Arlene wouldn't let her. She looked into Sheila's eyes and whispered, "Please. Please."

Sheila rocked forward. With her hands still in Arlene's, she lowered her head and held on tighter and the two of them wept softly, and if it took the whole rest of their lives Arlene wouldn't be the one to let go first.

LETTERS

H E HADN'T SEEN Derek since those mornings during the trial, riding in the transport van to the courthouse and back. On the first day they put their heads on each other's shoulders because they were cuffed, and Joel closed his eyes and leaned against Derek's forehead and breathed the yeasty scent of his scalp. Joel was told they'd get a visit at some point, since Derek was in a different block, but that hadn't happened and probably wouldn't for a while.

They put him in a cell next to an old-timer named Truvy, who was doing a life sentence for running down his girlfriend and some others while he was strung out on meth more than twenty years ago. There was a concrete wall between them, but Joel could hear Truvy hacking throughout the night, gagging on the blood that came up. The sound made Joel turn in his bunk, and sometimes to block it out he wrote letters he never sent. He tried to get his words right and sometimes he felt he did. But then by morning, when he read them again, those words, he realized, weren't what he'd meant at all. What seemed right in the darkness of his cell became something completely different in the day because in here the nighttime did something to your brain. You didn't need windows to tell the difference between the two. The night crept up on you all day long, and when it came and you lay on your bunk, it sat on your chest as a reminder that one more day had disappeared without ever being lived. The sound of his own breathing, the long moans from across the block. Some nights he heard screaming fits like the ones Sam had a few years ago, night terrors, where he wasn't quite awake or asleep. Screams like that could go on for a long time, and a few nights he found himself screaming alongside the sound. Then the noise would stop and the quiet would come back hard enough to give him chills.

Sometimes he dreamed of being suffocated. It was the smell of this place, that same air circulated over and over and the smell of bodies like in a nursing home, shit and vomit and piss all washed over with bleach. He could taste the coppery stench around him. That smell made him breathe shallow all day long, and there were nights he would stop breathing altogether. He would wake to find himself bolt-upright and gasping for air.

If he could see Derek it would make a difference. He hoped that when Derek was out he'd come see Joel so he'd know he was okay, and that even if Derek hated him they were still brothers. He could live with hate, even from Derek, but he couldn't stand knowing that Derek no longer took him as his brother, because that would mean there was nothing left for him at all.

The outside seemed farther away all the time. He could barely imagine himself in it anymore because even his dreams suffocated in here. The closest he could come were still moments, like photographs: touching the top of Sam's head, pressing his face between Lynn's breasts, inhaling the scent of her body. He missed her more inside, even if he knew it wasn't real. It was this place that was making him want her. The smallest thing in here could turn him on, the softness of his pillow, the smell of soap.

He tried not to think of the outside at all because it always made him wrestle with what he'd done. Whenever he tried to remember that kid's face it was like looking through a dirty window. He could see him twitching on the ground—he was twitching—but he still couldn't make out the kid's face, and no blood, which was strange. How could that be? Head trauma, they'd said, everything internal, his skull fractured, filling with enough blood to drown his brain.

He couldn't shake the girl, either, the one at the park that day. At night he saw her standing outside his cell with a face like one of those old ceramic dolls. The thought of her turned his stomach enough to make him dry heave off the side of his bunk because he'd hurt her too, every bit as bad as he'd hurt that kid, only she still had to live with that hurt.

It was Reed, the pastor, who got him to write down his thoughts. He came on Wednesdays, and even the hardest guys in this place were willing to talk to him because at least it was someone to talk to. Early on Joel tried to stay away because the guy made him nervous. He had tiny hands and a bushy mustache and a horribly twisted spine, and he seemed at ease all the time, which didn't make sense in this place. No one was at ease here, not the inmates or the C.O.s. If you were, it meant you were stupid or out of your fucking mind. For weeks the guy watched Joel, and one day Joel turned to find Reed sitting beside him.

After a while Joel said, "I'm not gonna talk to you."

"That's your choice," Reed said. His voice was nasally, elf-like.

"It's not going to do any good. I don't want to talk about God. It won't work for me."

"Who said anything about God?"

"I know what you are. That's where it always ends up."

"There are no rules when it comes to this sort of thing. But I figure there are things you need to say."

"I don't have anything to say. Nothing I say is going to change a thing."

Reed faced him. "I think you're wrong about that. Everybody needs to talk. Especially in here."

"I'm not any good at talking. Things don't come out the way I mean them to."

"Maybe you should say it without talking, then."

"What's that mean?"

"Write it down. Say what you have to on the page."

Joel shook his head. "I'm not any good at writing, either."

"Seems to me the least you can do is try."

He did try. He wrote to his mother and Derek and Lynn, and to Sam for when he was old enough to understand. If he was a writer, a real writer, he would know what to say. But saying he was sorry and that he never meant for any of it and that he'd switch places with that kid if he could, all that sounded like shit even though it was true. It sounded like what anyone would say. What he wanted to do was write a letter telling Sam that everything would be okay, that all the wrong he had done didn't mean Sam couldn't have a good life. But if he had received a letter like that when he was a boy it wouldn't have changed the fact that he was going to wind up here. He realized that now, that he was coming to this place one way or another and it was only because of himself, because he couldn't manage the stuff going on inside his own head, and when that happens and you don't get yourself killed this is where you end up.

He couldn't see the kid's face even if he closed his eyes and tried hard, and that scared him, because he knew that memory was still in his brain, hiding like a cancer in remission, there but not there, and one day it was going to come out and he was afraid of what would happen after that. Because even though he was to blame, it wasn't really him. That had to be true. If it wasn't it would mean he could have stopped and that kid would still be alive and Joel would still have a life and Sam would still have a daddy, so why wouldn't he have stopped it if he could? What kind of person wouldn't have stopped it if he could?

If he were a writer he could write to the kid's family and say what he felt, that he was sorry and that he hoped, really hoped, they never forgave him. It was hate that he deserved. The thought of forgiveness scared him more than being in this place and the beat-downs and the loneliness that hollowed out every part of him, so much that if he thought about forgiveness long enough he would start to shake right there in his bunk and cry out when he was wide awake without even realizing it. Then he'd have to live every last second of this miserable life carrying that kid around on his back and knowing that the kid's family still didn't hate him, didn't wish him any harm after what he did, and he'd know they were strong enough and good enough to not hate even after the worst kind of hurt, and that he couldn't say the same, and nothing would be worse than that. If he were a writer he could write them a letter and explain all that to them. A writer could say it and have it make sense.

In the cell beside his, Truvy was making hacking noises from all the way down in his gut, a wet barking sound that seemed like it would never end. One night Truvy was going to die in this place, hacking up the last of the poison inside him, and when there was nothing left to bring up an artery was going to let loose in his brain and bleed him out, and that was a terrifying thought, because when that happened the only thing left would be the sound of Joel's own breathing. In and out, in and out.

ESCAPES

ON THEIR LAST MORNING together Arlene took Sam to the Langley Recreation Center for a swim, just the two of them. Arlene sat on the steps by the shallow end as Sam splashed around her. Earlier in the summer he enjoyed the inflatable Spiderman swimmies she'd gotten him, but now he refused to wear them. He was already becoming self-aware, concerned with how he'd be seen by the other kids.

She was going to miss seeing him every day, Lynn too. From the time they had moved into the house Arlene felt insulated, safe. Strange how a tragedy could do that. It came, she supposed, from knowing that other people felt the same deep sorrow you did, that you weren't alone. The house felt brighter with them there.

Before they moved in, Arlene decorated Derek's room for Sam. She took down the old posters—Indie cars and bikinied women—and replaced them with spaceship decals she'd gotten from the dollar store. She bought a new bedspread with smiling, lime-green frogs and moved all of Derek's things into the bedroom closet. She would put them back when he came home—three more months on the aggravated assault charge—but Derek had told her not to bother. Something was extinguished inside him now. He didn't want anything the way it was and she wondered if he'd ever set foot in that house again. The last time she'd seen him he was thin in a way that looked unhealthy, and there was a dullness in his eyes that frightened her, as if they were disconnected from his mind and could never be reattached.

Lynn had been sleeping in Joel's room all these months. The first week she painted the walls a soft yellow that made the room feel fresh. Joel's musk was replaced with the scent of skin lotion.

They had somehow managed to cleanse the house.

Sam was racing a little girl across the width of the pool, the two of them dog-paddling and bouncing on their toes. About mid-way Sam swallowed a mouthful of water and let out an alarming belch-like cough. Arlene stood.

"Are you okay?"

He coughed a few more times and moved towards her.

"It's time, buddy. We have to head back."

"A few more minutes," he said with trembling purple lips.

"We have to get you on the road. Your mom is waiting for us." She went to the deck chair and pulled a towel from her bag, and when she returned to the stairs he was gone.

"Sam," she said.

The little girl held her nose and was about to go back under water when Arlene stopped her.

"Where did he go?"

She walked along the edge of the water and scanned the length of the pool. "Sam," she called, and spotted a child curled and motionless at the bottom. "Sam," she called again.

The child, an older boy, rocketed towards the surface and swam to the other end of the pool, and right then Sam appeared at her side.

"My God." She put her arms around him. His skin was slick and cold and she could feel the rise and fall of his birdlike chest. "You frightened me."

"I was right there, Nana." He pointed to a ring of shade beneath one of the umbrellas.

"It's okay." She wrapped the towel around his shoulders and rubbed his body and took him in her arms once again. "We're okay."

On the ride home they went by the new construction site. They had razed the old elementary school to make way for a housing complex. Neither of her boys had gone there, yet it still made Arlene sad whenever she passed. The school had been there her entire life and now it was about to vanish. Soon people would forget it had ever existed. She had become nostalgic for even the elements of life that meant little to her.

"It's almost gone, Nana," Sam said from the back seat.

"The machines are chomping it up." She clacked her teeth in the rearview mirror.

"There's an excavator. And a front loader."

"How do you know that?"

"I don't know, Nana. I just know it."

"You're a smart boy, you know that? My grandson is a smart boy."

She could see him twisting his body to get one last glimpse of the machines through the perimeter fence. He had the same curiosity Joel had as a boy.

She had last seen him only weeks before, not long after the judge handed him a twenty-five year sentence. They barely spoke. Arlene watched him through the glass, bent forward as if to hide his face. His head was shaved close enough to expose the wine-colored birthmark above his ear that she hadn't seen since he was a baby. He looked sad yet peaceful, somehow, resigned, as if he'd worked through stages the way you do with death and had finally reached acceptance. Arlene told him Sam was doing okay and that he missed his daddy, and Joel came back to life, not quite smiling but taking on a dreamy sort of look that she hoped would stay with him. When their time was up he looked into her eyes, with tenderness, she felt.

He said, "Tell him his dad is with him. Every day. Make sure he knows that."

At home Lynn's car was parked in front of the house with the box trailer hitched to the back. They'd spent the previous day loading it up themselves, she and Lynn alone, while Sam climbed over the boxes. Arlene was nervous about them leaving. They would be okay, she was certain, but she had never lived in the house alone before. What if it closed in on her? What would being alone do to her mind?

Inside, Arlene turned on cartoons for Sam. She made him a jelly sandwich (he hated peanut butter) and let him eat on the living room floor. She got down beside him.

"What are we watching over here?" she said.

"Scooby Doo," he said in a trance, holding a small, crustless square of sandwich beneath his chin.

During the commercial he leaned against her. He was much more affectionate than her boys. He would come to her sometimes and press himself against her side, and if she lifted him up he'd rest his head on her shoulder and grip the fabric of her shirt. He didn't have that shadow of discontent she remembered in her boys, where they resisted her touch, especially as they grew older.

Sam had a lump on his forehead from the day before. He had tripped over one of the boxes and whacked his head on the end table. It was beginning to bruise at the edges, and she touched the tender knot with her fingertips to see if the swelling had gone down.

"Are you coming with us today?" Sam said.

"No, honey. We talked about this. I'll come visit you soon, though."

"We can go to the beach."

"And you'll be starting school. Are you excited to be with the other kids?"

He nodded but his attention was on a television commercial that had kids jumping through a plastic lawn sprinkler. Behind her Lynn came down the stairs with a suitcase in hand and a large bag hanging from her shoulder. She set everything down and stood in front of Arlene, smoothing the wrinkles in her shorts.

"I think that's everything," she said.

She flipped her hair out from her collar and looked around the room to take inventory.

"I packed you some snacks for the ride," Arlene said.

"You shouldn't be sitting on the floor like that," Lynn said.

She held out a hand to help Arlene to her feet.

"He'll probably sleep in the car. He wore himself out pretty good this morning."

Lynn smiled to cover everything that was going on inside her. She scanned the room again.

"I didn't expect it to be so difficult. Even the bad stuff is hard to leave." She put a hand on her stomach like she was about to be sick. "Tell me I'm doing the right thing."

"It's going to be okay," Arlene said. "It really is."

"I couldn't have done this alone. Really. God knows how I would have gotten through the last year. At least you'll get some peace and quiet around here for a change."

"I can't say I'm much looking forward to that. Houses are supposed to have noise. My daddy used to say quiet is for churches and libraries, not the home. Took me all these years to understand that."

Lynn smiled weakly. She patted her pockets as if she'd lost something and handed Arlene a folded piece of paper. In barely a whisper she mouthed, "He's worried Joel won't know where we are. Last night he had me write this."

To Daddy, We are going to live in Florida. I will be at school sometimes but you can come see me when you are good. I love you. From Sam.

Arlene folded the letter quickly and stuffed it in her pocket so Lynn wouldn't have to see it again. She couldn't imagine ever giving it to Joel, and throwing it away felt like a betrayal to Sam. She would quarantine it instead, hide it away where it would be removed from their thoughts for good.

Lynn crouched down and tugged on Sam's ear and he snapped to.

"Come here, you. Let me get a hug."

She took him in her arms and carefully examined the lump on his head. "That's a nice goose egg you got there. We're gonna trade you back to the Gypsies, you know that?"

Sam rested his forehead against hers.

Outside they loaded the last bags into the trailer and Sam secured the padlock. Arlene watched him climb into the back seat and buckle himself in. She closed his door and rested her arms on the window jamb.

"Call me tonight so I know you're okay."

"Say, 'we will, Nana.'"

Lynn looked at Arlene and crimped her lips tight and Arlene nodded and Lynn did too. She started the engine and lifted her hand in the air.

"Okay, buddy," she said. "You ready, you set?"

Sam reached up and slapped her hand, then again.

"I'm go," he said.

ACKNOWLEDGMENTS

I would like to thank the following people for their generous support and help with the book: Tim Parrish, Wayne Harrison, Margot Livesey, DeWitt Henry, Andy Vogel, Alex Pierpaoli, Alla Budur, Jessica Ratigan, Andrea Dupree, Jenny Itell, and Eric Sasson. Thank you to Kutztown University for granting me sabbatical leave, which allowed me to finish the book, to the Prairie Center of the Arts Residency, Bread Loaf Writers' Conference, Sewanee Writers' Conference, Aspen Summer Words, and Lighthouse Writers Workshop for help with revisions, and to The Woven Tale Press for publishing the *Returns* chapter. And thank you to my parents, Ann and Richard Voccola, to my family, and especially to Melissa Papianou, for her feedback and careful edits, her patience and support, for everything.

Printed in the USA
CPSIA information can be obtained
at www.ICGtesting.com
LVHW052241050124
768158LV00003B/255